Elephant Ben

Geoffrey Malone spent most of his childhood in Africa and avoided any formal education until the age of eleven. After school in England, he spent sixteen years as a soldier, then joined a Canadian public relations firm in Toronto. During all this time, he travelled widely and developed a fascination with animals in the wild. He returned to Britain in 1991, determined to become a children's author.

He has written six books for children, each one with a powerful and closely-observed animal interest. His story of a fox, *Torn Ear*, won the 2001 French Children's Book of the Year Award and the Prix Enfants grands-parents Européen. In England, *Elephant Ben* was shortlisted for the 2001 Stockton Children's Book of the Year Award.

To get the background for this book, he spent over a year researching and observing at first hand, both elephants and the illegal trade in ivory poaching.

Elephant
Ben

GEOFFREY MALONE

Hodder
Children's
Books

a division of Hodder Headline Limited

ISBN 0 340 86059 6

Typeset by Avon Dataset Ltd, Bidford-on-Avon, Warks

Printed and bound in Great Britain by
Bookmarque

Hodder Children's Books
a division of Hodder Headline Limited
338 Euston Road
London NW1 3BH

To Richard, Susan and Katherine,
with love

One

Ben was late for supper. He was hungry and in a hurry. And this made him careless. He didn't see the snake until the last moment.

A sudden flicker of movement caught his eye. He glanced up at the huge ant hill that towered over the path and came to a frantic, sliding stop. He fell over in a cloud of dust and small stones.

There was blood all over his knee but he ignored it. He was too busy staring at the hole high up on the side of the mound. The sound of his mother's voice, shouting for him to come home, faded away. Now there was just him and the snake.

Two metres above him the snake's head gleamed in the bright evening light. Ben froze. There was no mistaking the brilliant green of its scales and those large eyes that looked far too big for its head.

The boy swallowed. The snake was a boomslang, which Ben knew was a bad-tempered killer that dropped down on its prey. One of his father's game-wardens had been bitten by one the year before. He had died two days later in hospital, the snake's venom clogging the flow of blood to his heart and liver.

The snake began to slide further out of its hole. Ben forced himself to keep perfectly still while its head swayed from side to side, peering down at him.

For a moment its eyes met the boy's. They were black and glistening and they seemed to look right through him. He felt the fear gathering between his shoulder blades.

The snake's tongue flickered again, gathering information from the hot, dusty air. It was not yet aware of the boy. If it had been, it would now be hissing open-mouthed in deadly warning.

Ben guessed that the heat waves along the surface of the ant hill were masking his presence. But for how long? He fought back the urge to scramble to his feet and make a run for it. The snake was far too quick and, besides, he could feel the strength draining from his legs.

2

His forehead was suddenly covered with sweat. There was nothing he could do to stop it. It began to sting his eyes. He blinked and lost sight of the snake. Panic rose in the back of his throat. His hands trembled. All he wanted to do was to grind them into his eyes and rub them until he could see!

He blinked furiously and by a miracle they cleared. He found the boomslang lying motionless above him, enjoying the warmth of the sun. Ben was trapped! The slightest move now would bring the snake rearing up, ready to strike.

Ben had learned a lot about snakes from his father, David Sitole. In his father's last posting, the game-warden's quarters were old and run-down and the thatched roof was full of snakes. Many nights he had lain awake shivering in his bed, listening to them hunting rats.

Wide-eyed he had followed their slitherings above the bedroom ceiling. Sometimes, when he had been very young, he had shouted for his parents.

But he was twelve now and far too sensible to be frightened like that anymore. Besides, his father had been promoted and they had moved to a different area. There were still a lot of snakes in the surrounding bush but their new house was made of brick and had a modern tiled roof.

The snake was moving again. Something had alerted it. With a strong twisting of its coils, it gathered itself into a tight knot then flowed silently down the side of the mound away from him.

Ben raised his head and saw why. He caught his breath. A tiny bush mouse was scurrying across the ground along the bottom of the ant hill. The snake had seen it and was in pursuit.

The mouse rarely ventured out in the daytime. But she was hungry and exhausted. She had a family of six babies safely hidden under the root of a nearby thorn bush.

For the past half hour she had been feeding them until the gnawing emptiness in her own belly had become unbearable. She had made herself wait until her family were all fed before slipping out to look for grass seeds.

Moments after she left the nest, she picked up the smell of food and ran towards it. She found a piece of fruit just dropped by a passing bird. It was so fresh that even the ants had not yet found it. The mouse seized it between her paws and began to nibble. It was delicious and she could think of nothing else.

It was a mistake she would never repeat. The snake's tongue flickered in excitement. Its head swung round. With infinite care, it began to slip down the ant hill, the scales along its belly silently powering it towards its prey.

The mouse finished eating and licked her paws. She sat up and began to clean her whiskers. When she had finished, she shook herself and puffed out her fur. She started to scratch.

Too late, the mouse felt the sudden gush of damp air as the snake's mouth opened. She squeaked once and was gone. For a split second, Ben saw the gleam of fangs, then the mouse was a twitching wet bundle in the snake's mouth.

Holding his breath, Ben stood up. He had pins and needles in one leg. He waited. The snake was moving quickly now towards a pile of stones. It disappeared into them. Ben took a step backwards. Then another. He was shaking from head to foot. He took a couple of deep breaths then set off for home at a clumsy run.

David Sitole braked the Land-rover to a gentle halt and reached for his field glasses. Elephants! A wide grin spread across his face. He had just spotted a family of them less than a kilometre away, following the valley below.

He got out and walked quickly away from the cloud of red dust that billowed up around the vehicle. David was a stockily built man with powerful arms and shoulders. Despite the day's dust and heat, his khaki uniform still looked smart.

He had always had a soft spot for elephants. He admired their intelligence and strength and the loyalty they had for their families. He could never understand why so many people, even some of his own staff, thought they all looked the same. 'Large and grey with big ears,' was how he had heard a tourist describe them recently.

To him, elephants were just as much individuals as people. Their bodies and faces were all quite different. Some had crumpled ears, some smooth; some were ripped. There were elephants with long tusks, short tusks, tusks that crossed over at the tips. There were strong resemblances within families, too.

Secretly, David preferred elephants to the majority of people he had met. But then he felt that about most animals.

He took cover behind a rock and carefully focussed the glasses. The elephants were trudging along in an untidy group. They looked tired and dispirited. David lifted the glasses and scanned back along the way they had come. There didn't appear to be a bull elephant following, which was unusual.

The family walked in companionable silence. Occasionally, they pulled clumps of grass up by the roots with their trunks and banged them against their legs to shake off the earth before stuffing them into their mouths.

He could see these elephants had come a long way. They were coated with several days' dust. They looked gaunt and hungry and their ribs were very visible. Their thick, leathery skin hung in deep folds which swayed as they walked.

They were led by an old matriarch with a magnificent pair of tusks which were at least a metre and a half long and probably weighed as much as thirty kilos each. One of her ears was badly torn. She was also lame in a front leg. Not surprising, he thought, considering she had to be all of fifty years old.

David knew that the other six adults would be her daughters and granddaughters. There were also three calves. Together, they all formed a clan which had existed for many generations.

The next biggest elephant was a fine looking female aged about twenty-five and fully grown. She was close to two and a half metres high at the shoulder and because of her size, was obviously second in importance to the matriarch herself. She had much smaller tusks and walked parallel with her mother a good thirty metres ahead of the rest of the family. She was followed by a six-month-old calf.

David watched them plod along and was puzzled by the way the old matriarch led her family from the far right-hand side of the valley. The usual place to lead from was the centre where her eldest daughter was.

He studied the two of them for some time before he realised that the old elephant was blind in her left eye. Her daughter was acting as a replacement.

As he watched, he saw the two of them turn their heads and raise their trunks in his direction. They would of course have heard the Land-rover long before he had spotted them.

Now they would have picked up his scent. Although their eyesight wasn't very good, David knew that their sense of smell was amazing. They were quite capable of picking up a man's scent from well over a kilometre away.

He looked at his watch. It would be sunset in an hour's time and he wanted to be home before the blackness of the tropical night closed in on him. Reluctantly, he pulled his binoculars over his head.

Kubwa, the matriarch, saw the flash and trumpeted to Temba, her eldest. Behind them, one of the younger mothers screamed for her calf. It ran to her and ducked down under her belly.

The herd stopped and watched David come round from behind the rock and stand looking down at them. Then he disappeared. They heard the engine start. Soon, they caught the choking smell of exhaust. It grew stronger. Temba bent her head and sucked up a trunkful of dust. She blew it high into the air, trumpeting in disgust.

Later, she saw the blue painted Land-rover crossing the ground some way in front of them. She flapped her huge ears in annoyance. She would remember it.

Two

Kubwa woke just after midnight. She always slept standing up these days. It took far too much effort to get back on her feet. Energy she didn't seem to have any more.

Around her, the rest of the family sighed and rumbled and slept. One of the calves was whimpering to itself. It would be hungry and very thirsty, Kubwa thought. They all were. She had not found water for two whole days. Not since she had led the family down off the slopes of the mountain and out of the acacia forest.

Some of the younger ones had not wanted to leave. There was shade in the forest and there was a stream to drink from. But Kubwa knew from bitter experience just how dangerous it was to stay there any longer.

The trees and the undergrowth were tinder dry. The forest was a vast fire trap waiting to ignite. And if that happened, a roaring curtain of flames would outrun them and encircle them. She had seen it happen to other herds and later found their bones charred and splintered by the heat.

So she had cuffed them with her trunk and turned in the direction of the great swamp, four days' march away. They had followed her, some still rumbling in protest. Temba brought up the rear to help chivvy them along.

Now, the night air was cool. It was the best time to walk. Kubwa would halt before midday and hope to find shade for the afternoon.

She looked across to where Temba lay sleeping and quietly called. Temba woke immediately and came to stand beside her. Mother and daughter touched each other's faces and heads with the tips of their trunks in affection.

Kubwa and Temba looked at the stars and smelt the air. The night was alive with sounds. Fruit bats squeaked and swooped across the elephants' backs. A family of wart-hogs was busy digging but stopped abruptly when a leopard sneezed near them. Panic-stricken, they ran for their burrow, the sound of their hooves echoing across the hard ground.

It was time to move on. Kubwa gave a low trumpet that brought the rest of the family clambering to their feet. For a minute the elephants stretched and yawned and took it in turns to rub each other's heads in greeting.

They always did this even if they had only been separated for a brief space of time. It helped bond them together as a family. When the adults had finished greeting one another, it was the turn of the calves. When it was over, the calves dodged in and out of the herd in pure excitement.

Temba called Moto to her. He was her first-born calf. He was six months old and weighed almost two hundred kilos. She loved him with a fierce tenderness she had never known before.

He ran up to her now and grasped her huge trunk with his little one. She fussed over him and told him to walk between her forelegs. It was far too dangerous to let him go off on his own. There were lions around. The family had listened to them roaring soon after the moon rose. A young calf on its own would be easy prey.

Kubwa waited until all the calves were safely with their mothers then, with her trunk swinging from side to side, she led them through the darkness and on towards the Great M'lumba Swamp.

An hour later, Temba stopped in her tracks. Kubwa walked over to join her. They stood together listening hard. Behind them, the others waited patiently.

There was a new scent on the air. A sickly sweet smell that every animal instinctively knows belongs to Man. Cautiously, they took stock. There were other scents too. Goats and dogs for a start.

The elephants hated dogs even more than they hated the columns of driver ants which sometimes swarmed up their sides and infested their eyes and ears. Dogs were Man's ally. Their loyalty was to him alone.

And then they caught the very faintest of scents that brought saliva dribbling into the back of their mouths. Water!

The rest of the family had sensed it too. They pushed forward, jostling each other. Kubwa ordered total silence and went on ahead to investigate. Like giant grey ghosts, the elephants followed. No human ear could guess they were coming. Their huge feet made no sound. Not a twig cracked nor a branch broke. The calves huddled closer to their mothers' legs.

A kilometre further on, Temba and Kubwa stepped out of the bush on to a stretch of open road. It gleamed white in the moonlight. Facing them was a high wire fence stretched tautly between thick wooden posts positioned every few metres. Beyond it, was a village.

It had been two years since the family had last been this way and in that time Man had been busy. This was a government-built settlement. A show-piece development sited squarely across Kubwa's old trail.

Kubwa and Temba went up to the fence. It reached a little way above their heads. There were thick rolls of barbed wire along the top of it and pegged to the ground inside. They examined it closely and found that the wire barbs were nothing like as long or as sharp as acacia thorns. Temba watched Kubwa lean against the fence and test its strength.

It was an effective obstacle for buffalo or lions but not for an elephant. However, there was no point them simply pushing it over. The noise would wake the dogs and they would immediately alert the men.

And all this time, the smell of water was growing stronger. It was tantalisingly close. Temba walked up and down the fence touching it with her trunk and looking for a safe way in.

She lowered her head and gently pushed against one of the supports. That gave her an idea. She wrapped her trunk around one of the posts and lifted. She felt a tremor running all the way down to its base a metre below ground.

She took a fresh grasp and, this time, bent her knees. She felt it stir, then slowly come free. She lifted it clear and placed it soundlessly against the wire.

Temba pulled out nine more posts before she was satisfied. Silently, they passed through the gap and threaded their way between the rows of neat little houses.

A nightjar saw them coming and flew off on silent wings. The frogs ignored them and went on with their croaking. Far away, a jackal called to its mate. But the dogs heard nothing.

The water tank was open-topped. It had a brick base and hose pipes snaked away into the darkness. They lined up along two sides and drank greedily, sucking up water into their trunks and pouring it deep down into their throats. Temba drank over eighty litres before she was satisfied.

When they had finished, they fanned out into the fields beyond, where in total contrast to their usual eating habits, they ate silently and quickly.

They stuffed ripe maize into their mouths until they had stripped the crop. They moved on to the banana trees, twisted off the heavy stems and laid them on the ground. Then they delicately picked individual bananas and ate them with great enjoyment.

Their appetites were colossal. Even Kubwa, as old as she was, still ate at least fifty kilos of vegetation each day. Her daughters could easily eat double that amount. When they had finished the bananas, they plundered beds of sweet potatoes and beans.

But dawn was coming and Kubwa wanted to put many miles between themselves and the village by daybreak. As the first cockerels stretched and pecked stiff-legged in the dust, the elephants faded away into the gloom.

Clear of the fence, they broke into a fast walk leaving behind them a scene of devastation and ruin.

Later that morning, a battered taxi pulled up beside a bar. A small, aggressive looking man got out and looked quickly around. He paid off the driver then ran up a couple of rickety steps and went inside.

He stood for a moment in the doorway, letting his eyes get used to the gloom. Behind him a bead curtain swayed and rattled. The men at the bar turned to look. Their laughter died away. The barman's eyes widened. He picked up a cloth and pretended to be busy wiping down the counter.

'I want a beer!' the little man ordered. 'In a glass!'

'Yes Mr Ruhl Sir! In a glass,' the barman echoed, looking flustered.

The two men sitting at the bar pretended to find something interesting at the bottom of their glasses. They drained them and left.

Ruhl went over to a table in the corner. 'Star!' he greeted the shadowy figure sitting there. 'You made good time. Business slow these days?'

Star shrugged. He was tall and had long slender fingers. 'You said it was urgent. That means only one thing. Money! Big money!'

The barman brought over Ruhl's beer. He started collecting old bottles from a nearby table.

'Leave that!' Ruhl ordered. The barman scuttled away. 'And turn the radio on!' Ruhl shouted after him. 'Loud!'

'So what's all the rush?' Star asked. He had a

quiet, singsong way of talking. 'What's the deal?'

Ruhl grinned. 'Got a fax yesterday. Our old friends in the Yemen. Guess what they want?'

Star considered. 'Rhino horn?'

'Even better.' Ruhl beckoned him closer. 'Ivory. A hundred kilos of it. Right away. Special client of theirs out East. They'll pay top rates.'

Star sat back and stirred his coffee. His face was expressionless. 'Times have changed my friend,' he said after a pause. 'It's ten years' prison these days. And they've got helicopters and armed wardens. My boys won't be too keen.'

Ruhl swore and banged his fist on the table. 'You gone crazy?' he demanded. 'Let me tell you something. The wardens are just a bunch of old farmers with rusty guns. With about five rounds of ammunition between the lot of them.' He glared at Star, waiting for a response. 'So what's the matter?' he jeered. 'Lost your nerve? Slowing up?'

Star sat very still. A fly landed on the table between them. Star's hand moved in a blur. He opened his palm and pulled off a wing. The fly buzzed around in a circle, its legs kicking frantically. He thrust it under Ruhl's nose.

'The day I slow up, you've got problems,' he said

mildly. 'And I'm not hearing anything about money.'

Ruhl's tone changed. 'There's five thousand dollars for you and another thousand for your boys.'

Star considered. Ruhl watched him anxiously.

'Look,' he said persuasively. 'It'll be a quick in-and-out job. The rains are coming. No one's going to be expecting you. It'll be like a trip to the zoo.'

'I'll need to talk to my people first,' Star told him.

'Then do that! And fast!' Ruhl snapped. He picked up his empty glass and crushed the fly. 'So do we have a deal?' he demanded. 'Because if we have, I've got a lot to organise.'

Star smiled and put out his hand. 'Give me twenty-four hours,' he said.

Three

Ben's family always ate breakfast outside during the dry season. It was the best time of the day. The dust had settled during the night and the air felt fresh. The huge boulders on top of M'goma Hill stood out clearly in the early morning sunshine even though they were over four hours' drive away.

This morning however, there was tension over breakfast.

'He's not going anywhere. Not 'til he finishes that project they've given him for the holidays!' Ben's mother said firmly. 'When he's done that and done it well, then . . . OK . . . he can go with you.'

The Sitoles lived over a hundred miles from the nearest town and school. During term time, Ben boarded with an uncle and aunt who lived there.

'But Mum,' groaned Ben. 'It's so boring. It's all about the constitution or something. And you know we're going on safari in two days' time.' He put out a hand and touched his mother's arm. 'I promise I'll do it as soon as I get back. Honestly. Promise . . .'

'I did say we'd be off on Thursday,' David Sitole agreed.

'And that was before we got his report,' interrupted his mother, holding up the letter that had arrived the night before. She looked sharply at her husband. 'You want your son to grow up with an education don't you?'

There was a heavy silence. 'Your mother's quite right,' his father said after a pause. He looked at Ben. 'How long will it take you to do?'

Ben scowled. For weeks he'd thought of little else but going away with his father in the Land-rover for a whole week's safari. Camping out at night and cooking their food over a primus stove; studying animals and following the map. Brilliant! He'd intended spending the morning checking over the lists of things they were taking. But now this!

'He can start work on it right after we've cleared away the breakfast things,' said his mother firmly.

Gloomily, Ben bent over his bowl. His six-year-old sister, Hannah, made a face at him. He was too miserable even to bother replying.

Later, he sat in the family's white-washed living room and opened a school book. 'Our country is ruled by the President through a Council of Ministers,' he read. Ben gave a sigh and tried to concentrate . . .

Some time later he heard the radio crackle in his father's office and the sound of his voice answering. There was the loud scrape of a chair being pushed back and a shout.

David Sitole was buckling on his belt when Ben put his head round the door. His mother pushed past him. 'What's happened?' she cried.

His father shook his head. 'It's that new settlement. A herd of elephants broke in last night and destroyed their crops. That was the headman. He's demanding I go and shoot the entire herd or else he'll report me to the Minister.'

'But that's unfair! You warned them not to build the village there,' Mrs Sitole said indignantly.

David shrugged. 'Since when are animals more important than politics or property developers?' he asked angrily.

'You're not going to shoot the elephants, are you?' demanded Ben.

His father shook his head. 'The herd'll be miles away by now. Besides, it'll take me the best part of a day even to get there.'

'So how long will you be gone for?' his wife asked.

'Three days at least,' he told her. 'And if it is as bad as he says, I'll need a whole day to calm down the villagers. Poor people.'

'Can I come?' Ben asked hopefully.

His father shook his head and looked impatient. 'This is serious stuff, Ben. You just get that essay finished. Then we'll see about the safari.'

'Well, I just hope those elephants are a long way away, that's all,' Ben muttered. He went back to his books.

Temba burst through a dense patch of thorn bush and came to an abrupt halt. She lifted her trunk high in front of her like a periscope and smelt the air. There was danger ahead. She could feel it.

She had stopped in mid stride, one huge foot poised above the ground. Now, she put it gently down and listened. Clouds of flies buzzed round her eyes but she ignored them.

She turned her head from one side to the other trying to pinpoint exactly where the danger lurked and what shape it might take. She moved forward in total silence.

The others were some way behind her. They were ambling along, browsing on whatever vegetation they could find and grumbling about the lack of water. Yesterday's raid on the village was already only a memory.

They were all thirsty again, especially the calves and Kubwa. The old elephant was feeling the heat particularly badly. Temba had never known her suffer like this before. Her lameness was growing worse. As the sun climbed higher, she had even asked Temba to walk more slowly.

Watching her mother struggling on beside her, Temba knew it wouldn't be long before Kubwa handed over the leadership of the family to her. And that was something Temba wanted more than anything. A surge of elation ran through her at the thought. To disguise it, she ripped a branch off a tree and scratched the back of her neck with it.

But that all seemed a long time ago. Now, her concentration was centred on what lay ahead. She squinted into the heat haze, aware of a growing feeling of menace all round her.

She picked up the scent of a black rhino and a hundred metres further on, found a pile of its droppings. They were fresh. The sun hadn't yet dried them. The rhino had been along here within the past half hour.

She followed the path it had taken, noting the broken branches on either side and the deep scuff marks in the dust. The rhino had stopped beside a termite mound where it had marked its territory. There was rivalry between the two species over food and grazing. But a rhino was never any match in intelligence or strength for an elephant.

Temba continued on until she noticed a jumble of rocks a short distance ahead. They made a perfect place to watch from and her unease grew.

If only the rains would come and bring the vast herds of zebras and wildebeest with them. Then the predators would have all the food they wanted. As it was, they were starving and even more dangerous than usual.

Earlier that morning, the elephants had walked past a pack of hyenas cracking open the bones of an old buffalo they had pulled down during the night. They were too busy fighting amongst themselves to notice the family until the herd was almost upon them. When they did, the hyenas left the kill and ran snarling at the elephants to warn them off.

Kubwa had trumpeted at them in derision but afterwards none of the family could ever remember hyenas being so aggressive, especially when every animal on the plains knew that elephants were herbivores.

A little breeze suddenly sprang up out of nowhere and brushed the side of Temba's face. Gratefully, she turned towards it and caught the unmistakeable smell of lion.

It had been rolling in giraffe droppings but Temba was not so easily fooled. She stared hard at the rocks again. Lions were no real threat to her but there was Moto and the other two calves to consider.

Temba knew just how cunning lions could be. This might just be a solitary lion watching them, hoping to find an elephant calf wandering off on its own. Or it could be a deliberate trap laid by an entire pride and she was leading her family right into the middle of it.

She gave a bellow of warning, then called Moto to her. Behind her, she heard the other mothers calling and the answering cries of the calves.

There was a sudden loud squealing that made her blood run cold. She lurched round in disbelief and saw Moto running for his life, eyes rolling in terror and his little trunk jerking uncontrollably.

She saw the lioness at his heels and the muscles of her back legs already bunching for the leap.

Temba screamed and charged. Moto saw her and swerved in the nick of time just as the lioness sprang. She skidded across his back, slashing at his hide with outstretched claws trying to steady herself for the killer bite to his backbone.

Then she was rolling over and over across the ground, spitting with fury and skidding towards Temba in a cloud of dust.

Temba thundered towards her, roaring with hate. She slid the last five metres on her knees stabbing with her tusks and catching the lioness a glancing blow in the ribs as she struggled to her feet.

The lioness screamed in agony but somehow twisted away from under the next thrust. She dragged herself to her feet and ran off as fast as she could.

Another lion appeared. A young male with a thick mane. He crouched, staring at Temba, his tail lashing the ground. Moto's back was bleeding heavily. The

27

lion also smelt the blood. His eyes gleamed.

Behind her something else moved. Another lion! Temba swung round and saw a tawny shape disappear into the long grass. As she turned, the male lion made a short rush towards her. Then he hugged the ground motionless. Staring at her eyes.

The pride was after Moto. She knew that now for certain. The male roared. There were answering grunts from the scrub on either side of her. Temba was surrounded. She pounded the ground with her feet and trumpeted in distress.

The male moved closer. She caught the stench of his breath. Then Kubwa errupted out of the long grass and charged the lion with her huge ears spread wide and her tusks gleaming.

The lion sprang to one side, slashing at Kubwa's face as she pivoted round in a sheet of sand and stones and came after him. Temba remembered the other lionesses in the nick of time and stayed where she was. The lion roared in frustration, dodged the next attack and ran off into the grass as the rest of the family came running.

When they were sure all the lions had gone, the elephants formed a circle around Temba. They soothed Moto and gently examined the claw marks with the tips of their trunks. The gashes along his back were deep but not life threatening. Temba knew she needed to pack them with mud. Already they were covered with blowflies.

The elephants leaned against each other, still very distressed. The younger ones had their tails curled high over their backs and their eyes rolled with fright.

Later, the entire family began to mill around, wrapping their trunks round each other and rubbing foreheads. Some of them spun round and round in circles, trampling the ground and sending up clouds of choking dust. The noise was deafening and the air full of screams and trumpetings and roars. Temba stabbed her tusks again and again into the ground.

It took a long time before they became calm. When at last they did so, Kubwa resumed the lead. Luck was with her. She found a clump of fever trees where they dozed for the entire afternoon out of the sun.

Kubwa thought they should reach the swamp by dawn the next day. As soon as it became cooler, they moved on and trudged through the night. As the sky flushed pink in the early dawn, Temba halted on top of a low ridge.

In the strengthening light, they saw the ground below them was green and lush with grass. There were flocks of birds swooping overhead and hippos watching them from wide pools of water. A leopard stopped drinking and lifted its head to stare at them.

They trumpeted in pleasure and followed Temba at a run down the slope. They had arrived. Now their worries were at an end!

Four

Star turned in his seat and shouted above the roar of the engine. 'When we get to the customs post, leave all the talking to me. Understand?'

The men nodded. Outside, bushes and clumps of bamboo flashed past in the light of the headlamps. Swarms of flying ants came whirling out of the night and spattered themselves against the windscreen. The wipers only made it worse.

'Watch the ditch!' Star yelled. There was a sudden crash and the vehicle lurched violently. The steering wheel whipped away from under Alvarez's grasp. Star banged his head hard against the side window.

The engine stalled, pitching the cursing men forward. Cooking pots clattered across the floorboards.

'Do that again and I'll kill you!' shouted one of the men in the back, sliding a huge hand round the driver's throat.

'Shut up, Seku!' Star ordered. 'Leave him!' He looked across at the driver. 'You're the worst damn driver in Africa, Alvarez. I should have left you to rot in that abbatoir.'

Alvarez grinned and restarted the engine. The back wheels spun. The truck heaved and shook. Slowly, it righted itself and lurched back on to the road.

A mile further on, they saw lights ahead of them. 'Slow down,' Star warned. 'And remember, leave it to me.' They nodded, only too happy to agree.

The customs post was a small brick building with a corrugated iron roof. There was a faded sign above a sagging wall of old sandbags. A television set flickered inside.

'Dim your lights,' Star said quietly as they approached. They stopped in front of a white painted barrier that straddled the road.

A soldier watched them from a doorway. He waited until the dust had settled, then strolled over. He switched on a large torch and shone it into Star's face. Star smiled politely into the glare.

'Where you going?' the soldier demanded.

Star told him.

'Why?' asked the soldier.

'My brother's getting married,' Star confided. 'These people here are my cousins,' he added, jerking a thumb over his shoulder. The soldier held the torch up and flashed it over their faces. He looked uncertain and began to back away.

'Sergeant!' he shouted. The rifle slipped off his shoulder. He made a grab for it, dropping the torch in the dust as he did so.

The sergeant appeared at the doorway, peering out at them. Star noticed that the flap on his holster was undone. The soldier shouted again. The sergeant strode importantly towards the vehicle.

'Good evening captain!' Star greeted him, with a slight bow of the head.

'Papers!' the sergeant demanded with an impatient flick of his fingers.

Star reached inside his shirt and drew out a well-thumbed passport. There were several crisp banknotes inside.

'We'd like everyone under your command to drink my brother's health,' he explained smoothly.

The sergeant said nothing. He pocketed the

money and handed the passport back to Star. He snatched the flashlight from the soldier, went round the back and peered inside the truck.

Star clambered down and followed him.

'What's in those boxes?' the sergeant demanded.

'Tins of corned beef,' Star told him. 'You know how poor they are over there.'

There was a sudden crackle of gunfire. Then the wailing of police sirens. The sergeant grunted. He waved Star away and hurried back to the television.

The soldier swung the barrier up and the truck drove through. The men in the back gave a whoop of triumph and slapped each other's upraised hands. 'Time to pick up the guns,' Star said with a smile.

They drove for another hour. Once, Alvarez had literally to stand on the brakes as a rhinoceros came blundering out of the bushes, fifty metres ahead of them. It stood in the middle of the road squinting at the headlights and turning its great head from side to side in bewilderment.

Alvarez gave a low whistle. 'Look at the size of that horn!' he exclaimed. 'That'd be worth a pile of dollars. And no one's got a gun!'

'Put your lights out,' Star ordered. 'And keep quiet the rest of you.'

'But we can't stop here!' Alvarez cried. 'What happens if the thing charges? I'm going to back up.'

Star put his hand on the wheel. 'Just do what I tell you ... then you might possibly live to middle age. OK?' The menace in his voice was unmistakeable. There was a long pause.

The animal's smell reached them. Alvarez wrinkled his nose and cleared the back of his throat. He spat out of the window.

The rhino snorted a couple of times. Then after what seemed an age, they saw its bulk moving against the blackness. It broke into a trot and they heard it crashing through the undergrowth on the other side of the road.

Star cupped his hand and looked at his watch. 'It'll be light in two hours. I want to be loaded and on our way long before then. Let's go!'

The village was in total darkness. 'Look for the petrol pumps,' Star reminded them. A dog raced towards them in the headlights. It ran alongside snapping at the wheels. Alvarez spun the wheel trying to run it over.

'There it is!' cried Star triumphantly. 'Fifty metres on the right.'

They turned down a track and stopped beside a long, low building. A wrecked car had been dumped in front of a steel door. Star took a coin from his pocket and rapped on it. They waited. There was a strong smell of drains.

'What's keeping him?' grumbled Seku, slapping at the mosquitoes.

A light flicked on. They heard the slip-slop of sandals approaching. A key turned in the lock and the door was pushed open.

A man's voice asked, 'Nobody following you?'

Star brushed past him. The others followed quickly. The man looked out into the night and listened for a while. Then he locked the door behind them. He was small and balding and wore a greasy vest. His stomach bulged over the top of his trousers.

His name was Pete and Star did not quite trust him. But he had worked for Ruhl for many years. Ruhl swore by him.

They followed him across the garage floor. A dead rat lay in a corner beside a leaking oil drum. The storeroom was lit by a solitary bulb.

Pete indicated a long wooden packing case. 'All

yours,' he said. They used tyre levers to prise up the planks while their shadows swooped crazily over the walls.

Inside, there were four waterproof packages. Alvarez took a long knife from inside his shirt and slashed at the coverings.

'Very nice,' purred Star moments later, cradling the Russian-made assault rifle in his arms. He cocked the weapon, pulled the trigger and felt the jar as the firing block slammed into the breech.

'Very nice,' he said again. 'Where's the ammunition?'

Pete indicated a row of boxes stacked along one wall.

'What about the radio?'

'It's in my office,' the small man told him. 'Already tuned to the warden's frequency. All you've got to do is switch on and listen.'

'What about fuel?' Alvarez asked. 'The truck's half empty.'

Pete nodded. 'There's a pile of jerricans round the back. Help yourself.' He turned to face Star. 'You got my money?'

Star took a wallet from an inside pocket. 'Any wardens or soldiers been around recently?' he asked, watching the man's lips move as he counted the money.

Pete shook his head.

'No sign of helicopters?' Star prompted.

The man looked surprised. 'Of course not! The rains'll be here any day now. Too much lightning and bad cloud. They wouldn't risk it.'

It was the longest speech Star had ever heard him make. He smiled down at him. 'Good! We'll be on our way then. See you in about two weeks.'

The man watched until the tail lights of their vehicle disappeared. Then he pulled the money out of his pocket and kissed it. A slow grin spread across his face.

He locked the door behind him and switched off the light. Within minutes he was asleep.

Ben opened his eyes, yawned and sat bolt upright. He hadn't been dreaming. He remembered. It was for real!

They were going on safari today! In only a couple of hours. He wondered what the time was and reached for the little alarm clock he had been given last birthday. Then he remembered the battery was dead.

He had meant to buy a new one from the school shop. Instead he had spent the money on a football magazine. He'd tell his mother. She wouldn't forget.

He threw back the sheet and padded to the window. Outside the trees were black against a glowing sky. It was that magical time when the sun hesitates below the horizon and all nature holds its breath, waiting for the day to begin.

Ben watched the sky fill with colour and saw the sun leap up into the sky and flood the land with light. The night was over.

His father's Land-rover was standing in the drive outside. There was a badly gashed tyre on top of the bonnet. Ben studied it. They'd need a new spare wheel. This one was too badly damaged to ever use again.

David Sitole had been in low spirits when he had arrived back. 'The government are going to have an elephant cull,' he told them as they sat down for an early supper. 'At least, that's the rumour I'm hearing.'

'But I thought they weren't allowed to do that any more,' his wife protested, ladling out a large helping of chicken and lentil stew. 'What about all those international agreements they keep on signing?'

David looked unhappy. 'The government needs

the money. And this is a guaranteed way of raising it. They can sell the ivory to the Far East again.'

'I bet that'll bring back all those poachers,' said Ben.

'Don't talk with your mouth full,' his mother admonished.

His father looked at him and nodded. 'You're right,' he said. 'The trouble is, it'll be popular. A lot of people want it. The folks in that village I went to, for a start.'

He stared round at his family and shook his head. 'There are too many people these days. They all need land. Just like the elephants. Trouble is, they both want the same bits!'

Later in the evening, he cheered up a little. 'How is the homework?' he asked.

'All finished,' Ben told him, grinning.

'He's done fine,' his mother smiled. 'Made sense to me, any rate.'

'He took lots of paper from your desk,' Hannah told them. 'I saw him. I told him not to!'

'And it's past your bedtime too,' Mrs Sitole told her. 'Say goodnight to everyone.'

'So can we go on safari?' Ben asked as soon as the others had left the room.

His father yawned and rubbed his eyes. 'Well,' he said slowly, 'I suppose if we don't go soon we never will. The way the clouds are building up, the rains will be here any day. Let's see what your mother says. I've a mind to go tomorrow. Can you be ready by then?'

Ben spluttered with excitement. For weeks he had been preparing for this moment. He grinned at his father.

When his mother returned, he took her by the hand and led her over to the sofa and sat beside her. 'Mum,' he said, trying to sound in control, 'Dad's got a very important question to ask you. Please say yes.'

Mrs Sitole looked from one to the other. 'Is it about him having extra maths coaching in the holidays?'

'No!' cried Ben, horrified.

'You want to help more around the house, then?'

Ben groaned. 'Be serious Mum!'

His father took pity on him and told her. To Ben's amazement all she said was, 'Just as long as he packs enough underpants and takes his washing things . . .'

Ben's whoops of joy drowned what else she had said. He grinned again at the memory. It was for real. Even so, he could still hardly believe it.

Now the sun was already hot on his face and the earth smelt fresh and inviting. He saw a rat run across the yard and down along the chicken run.

It would be looking for a hole to wriggle through to get at the eggs. Well, it would be unlucky, he thought. He had spent hours last week checking the wire. He clapped his hands and hissed after it.

The house was very still. No one else was awake. He wondered if he should get dressed and start loading the Land-rover.

He suddenly felt quite tired. His bed looked very inviting. He'd just lie down for a couple of minutes . . . and he was asleep again as his head touched the pillow.

Five

At about the same time, Kubwa was leading the family down to the swamp. They had already fed on a clump of low trees. Now they were all looking forward to their usual hour-long bathe.

The family were happy. The adults followed on one behind the other. Their trunks swung good-naturedly from side to side. The calves dodged in between them, reaching up with their little trunks and tugging at the bigger elephant's tails. Then they ran screaming with excitement into the bushes on either side.

Kubwa and Temba listened to the noise they made and hummed contentedly to themselves. The long thirsty march was forgotten. Kubwa had led them to water. Although the swamp was only a fraction of the size it would be when the rains came, there was still more than enough water for every animal.

Kubwa had shown Temba the landmarks to watch for when it came to be her turn to bring the family down off the mountain.

It was the best time of the day. It was cool and there was very little dust in the air. Their shadows slanted far in front of them across the parched ground.

At the top of a steep bank, Kubwa halted and waited for the family to catch up. The calves ran along the top peering down and protesting.

The adults milled around for a while then started to descend. Kubwa went first, holding on to the trunk of a tree to steady herself. Temba was next. She slid down on her haunches with her forelegs held stiffly out in front of her. At the bottom, she trumpeted with pleasure and turned to encourage Moto.

He slid down in a headlong rush, his trunk curled up on top of his head. She caught him and slowed him down. The two younger calves took more persuasion. They pressed against their mother's legs and squealed in fright.

In the end, with their mothers pushing and

Temba reaching up for them, they came down at a faltering run, screaming in protest. Afterwards, they swaggered up and down in relief and threw lumps of dried mud at Moto.

The cracked mud plain stretched away to a dark belt of reeds two kilometres away. The elephants spread out and ambled towards the distant swamp. Scores of lizards fanned out in front of them. A puff adder drew itself into a tight coil and lay motionless until long after they had passed.

Gradually the ground became softer and water began to seep in and cover their footprints. Soon a thick tangle of rushes closed over Temba's head as she tunnelled her way through. Millions of mosquitoes rose to greet her, biting at the thinner skin of her ears.

Then she was through and in the open again. She sank waist deep into cool, welcoming water. With a sigh of pleasure, she sucked up a trunkful of water and poured it into her mouth.

Temba drank steadily, filling her trunk four times before she was satisfied. Then she rolled over on her back, thrashing from side to side and enjoying the feel of water on her face.

She heaved herself upright and looked around.

Moto was close by, his head covered with weed. He was smacking the water with his trunk and kicking his legs backwards and forwards making huge splashes.

Temba sucked up another trunkful and blew water over him. All round them, the family drank and splashed and used their trunks as water hoses to spray each other. It was a wonderful game.

The elephants were not the only animals in the swamp. Near a ledge of low rock, a family of hippos watched and snorted in disapproval. This was their territory and the elephants were unwelcome visitors. They showed no respect for the hippos and splashed them and even sprayed them with their trunks.

The hippos were not used to being treated like this. Every other species in the swamp was careful not to disturb them. Even the crocodiles took care to keep out of their way. They knew that a bad-tempered bull hippo was quite capable of biting a crocodile in half if challenged.

Now, with their tiny ears bobbing up and down in annoyance, the hippos swam off towards a strip of sandy beach some distance away.

But on the ledge, something moved. A large, scaly head lifted and watched until the hippos were out of sight. When it was sure they had gone, the crocodile turned and stared unblinkingly at the elephants.

Ten minutes later, it found what it was looking for. Carefully, with hardly a ripple, it slipped into the water and began to drift down towards the family.

The crocodile's name was Kyrit. He was over four metres long and had lived in the swamp for thirty years. He had been waiting for the family to appear. He had watched Kubwa bring the elephants to this same spot at exactly the same time for the past three days.

He knew they were coming long before the marsh birds began calling. Like all the land animals he had studied, elephants were entirely predictable. Kyrit had also noticed that at this time of the morning, the early sun would be shining directly into their eyes.

The glare off the water was dazzling. That was why he had chosen the ledge to watch from. No one would see him getting really close until the very last moment.

So now, Kyrit let the current push him down towards the happy, trumpeting throng. And all the time he watched, waiting for the right moment.

The smallest calf in the herd was tired of being splashed by the others. She stood patiently waiting for the signal to leave. The water reached her shoulders and she carried the end of her trunk high above her head. It was an excellent aiming mark.

Moto and the other calf were becoming bored with her. It was no fun teasing her if she kept ignoring them. Eventually, they moved off. Her mother looked round, saw she was safe and went back to a long wallow.

The calf took a step towards the reeds. No one told her not to. She took another. And another. A gap was beginning to open.

It was exactly what Kyrit was waiting for. Smoothly he changed direction. A small furrow appeared on the surface of the water on either side of his long jaws.

The calf was moving with more assurance now. From ten metres away, Kyrit judged the spot where she would disappear into the reeds. He wanted to seize her just as she reached them, when her attention would be distracted. Then he could drag her under and drown her.

He dug deeper with his back legs and surged towards her. The calf was very close to the reeds now. Suddenly, she looked up and for an instant they stared at each other. Kyrit saw the sudden understanding in her eyes.

The calf whimpered. She knew she was in danger. She could see it racing towards her. She wanted to turn and run to her mother. But the water was holding her back. Instead, she slipped and lost her footing. She fell with her back to the crocodile.

An elephant screamed a warning. Kyrit heard it and accelerated. He swung his tail in two great heaves and came up out of the swamp with his jaws wide open.

The water boiled as the crocodile's teeth raked the calf's back, frantically trying to seize her and pull her under. But for once in his life, Kyrit had miscalculated. Her back was too wide and his jaws could not get proper hold.

All round him he knew the danger was growing. Huge legs were wading towards him. The water was alive with pounding feet and discordant screams. Kyrit clambered across the calf's back, a red rage misting his eyes.

The calf was rigid with fear. It was squealing. A high-pitched, bubbling cry. Furious, Kyrit forced the calf to her knees, battering at her with all his weight.

Her legs were buckling and the next moment she fell face forward. He could hear water rushing into her lungs. His jaws closed round her leg. The surface boiled as he began dragging her into deeper water. And then Temba's trunk seized his tail.

Kyrit fought with all his strength. He hung on until his jaws ached. But there was no escaping the elephant's remorseless grip. She was dragging him off.

He was in danger. Great danger. There were elephants all round him, cutting off his escape route. And he was tiring. There wasn't much time left.

Panic-stricken, Kyrit suddenly let go. Startled, Temba lost her grip. In a flash, Kyrit was free. Temba stumbled backwards, giving him the space he needed. Kyrit spun around and launched himself at her.

Now he was twisting in mid air, the claws on his back feet ripping at Temba's head and eyes. He hung there for a moment bellowing in fury.

But the elephant was too quick for him. She swung her head and her tusks caught him a terrible blow to the ribs. For a split second, the crocodile lay helpless on top of the water.

Temba splashed after him, wrapping her trunk

around his tail. She bent her legs and lifted the crocodile straight up. She whirled him round her head a couple of times then brought him smashing down with a terrible crack.

Kyrit landed on his back and lay there stunned, his feet kicking feebly. Kubwa shouldered past Temba. She placed a massive foot on the crocodile's belly and crushed him far down into the mud. She waited five minutes until two great bubbles of air came bursting to the surface, before letting go.

Afterwards, they plastered mud into the deep gouges along the calf's back and leg. This would keep out blowflies and stop the wounds from going septic.

All that morning, the calf shivered uncontrollably while they fussed over her. Moto and the other calf looked on in silence and stayed very close to their mothers.

By nightfall, the calf was better. It had begun to suckle again and the family knew it would be alive in the morning.

Six

Breakfast took forever. His mother insisted they all have boiled eggs. Ben hated eggs. The smell of them always made him feel sick. He made a mental note to make a hole in the chicken wire when they got back from safari.

But he couldn't be cross for long. As soon as breakfast was over, his father went to his office to call headquarters on the radio. Ben began to load the Land-rover. He had made long lists of the things they were going to need. The first and most important of these was water.

The Sitoles had their own water source deep underground. A bright red diesel pump brought it to the surface. Ben lined up four ten-litre plastic water carriers and filled them from a tap. It took all his strength to carry them out to the vehicle and lift them up on to the tailboard.

He was panting hard by the time he pushed the last one into its place under a seat and dropped the securing bar in place. That would stop them shifting round and becoming damaged.

Next, he checked that they had a good supply of water sterilisation tablets. His father had told him that the water in the cans would have to last them for three full days. And that was for everything – drinking, cooking and washing. After that, they would have to sterilise everything they drank.

That done, he went to the kitchen and brought back a cardboard box full of tin plates, cooking pots, knives, spoons and cooking oil. Then there were the ant-proof containers full of rice, dried beans, sugar, tea, jam, hard-tack biscuits, salt and raisins.

His mother came out holding a large vacuum flask. Ben stowed it carefully in a specially padded space between the front seats. David Sitole always insisted that hot sweet tea was the best thing to drink in really hot weather. It kept you cool because it made you sweat. And that stopped you from getting heat exhaustion. Most of the other wardens agreed with him. Ben preferred cold tins of cola. He was thrilled when his mother returned with an ice box full of them.

Ben went back with her to the kitchen where she gave him a large bag of homemade biltong: long strips of antelope meat, salted and dried in the sun until hard. Ben and his father would chew this throughout the day. It was nourishing and delicious and a great favourite of theirs.

When the supplies were all finally packed, they replaced the damaged spare wheel. David finished tightening the last securing bolt with a large spanner. 'Time to check the winch,' he told Ben. 'Remember what to do?'

Ben got behind the wheel of the Land-rover. He shook the gear stick to make sure it was in neutral and switched on the winch motor.

His father bent down by the front bumper and seized the winch hook. He then walked slowly backwards for ten metres, pulling the heavy tow wire after him. When it was fully extended, he signalled to Ben to come and join him.

They squatted down together and examined the cable for any signs of damage or fraying. 'Can't be too careful with winches,' he told Ben. 'I've seen worn ones snap and take a man's leg off at the knee.

Your life can depend on one of these things. So look after it. You never know when you might need it!'

They spent another twenty minutes checking the first-aid kit and making sure Ben had packed the tent pegs and a mallet. The tent itself was an old army one. It was heavy and made of very stiff canvas. It took a lot of effort to push it up on to the roof.

'Why don't you get a new tent, Dad?' Ben demanded when it was finally stowed. 'You can buy really lightweight ones these days. They have them at school.'

David peered down at him and made a face. 'Yes! And I've seen them after they've been out in the bush for a week,' he scoffed. 'Ripped to shreds! This one of ours is thorn-proof, waterproof and just about lion-proof.' He wiped the sweat from his face. 'And that's a big plus for where we're going!'

At last, they were ready. 'Look after him,' he heard his mother say. 'And you do exactly what your father tells you, you hear me!' she told Ben. 'It's a wild place out there. I must be crazy letting you go.'

As Ben kissed her goodbye, she pressed a small package into his hand. 'Keep it safe in your pocket,' she told him and hugged him again.

Ben tore open the paper and gasped. 'Fantastic!

Thanks Mum. It's great!' and he held up the gleaming Swiss Army penknife for his father to see.

'Mind the blades now,' she called after him. 'They're really sharp.'

The engine started, Ben jumped in and a moment later they swung out on to the track that ran past their house. Hannah and his mother waved and watched until they were swallowed up in the vast silence.

They drove for two hours across the rolling plains while the sun climbed vertically into a blue sky and a heat haze danced in front of them.

David pointed to a solitary tree a kilometre away. 'We'll stop there for a break. Have some tea,' he said. 'Unless there's lion around. Keep your eyes open.'

Ben stared at the chest-high yellow grass. A thousand lions could hide here and no one would ever know, he thought.

'Never park under a tree if you can't see what's up in the branches,' David told him as they drew closer. 'Might be a big hungry leopard waiting up there.'

'Aah!' he exclaimed. 'There's been something big here all right. Take a look!' All round the tree the grass had been flattened. Cautiously, David got out.

He came round the front of the vehicle and stood beside Ben's door. 'Smell anything familiar?' he asked.

'That's lion,' he went on. 'Never forget it.' He clambered up on top of the bonnet and looked around. 'OK. Come on out Ben,' he called. 'And bring the flask.'

It was a brilliant moment, Ben thought. Drinking tea like this in the open while his father interpreted the signs.

'There was a lion sleeping here last night,' David said. 'See those scratch marks on the tree? Look how fresh they are. Solitary male, I'd guess. Too young to have his own pride yet. Trying to stake out his territory. Won't do him much good round here though.'

'Why not?' asked Ben.

'This is Black Mane's patch. I've told you about him before. Remember? Biggest lion I've ever seen. He'll send this one packing in no time.'

They finished their tea. It was good to wash the dust out of their mouths. As they got back into the Land-rover again, David pointed at the horizon. 'See that little cloud?' he asked. 'In a couple of hours it'll cover the whole sky.'

'Will it rain?' Ben wanted to know.

His father nodded. 'It will some time this week. We'd better get on. I want to be at the swamp by tomorrow. That's where all the animals go. Like to drive for a bit? There's not much for you to bump into out here. You'll be fine.'

By mid-afternoon, they were driving through quite different country. They were coming down off the plain through a range of low hills. Now there were steep-sided gullies to cross where they bounced and crashed over sharp rocks and spun their wheels in patches of loose sand. The air hung motionless and it was too hot even for the scorpions.

There was a smell of stale electricity in the air. And all the time, the clouds pressed down and it grew darker. Soon they were driving on full headlights. There was a brilliant flash of lightning and a colossal clap of thunder which made Ben bite his tongue.

The next moment they were driving into a solid curtain of water that stopped the wipers. They waited for ten minutes while the rain hammered on the roof and streamed in through the joints in the doors.

Then, just as suddenly, it stopped, leaving a

rainbow and red mud everywhere. By sundown, the ground was almost dry again. They stopped on top of a low ridge and saw the gleam of the swamp, three kilometres further on.

'Perfect,' said David. 'This will do us nicely. Let's get the tent up and some food on. Don't know about you but I'm starving.'

They had often practised putting up the tent back at home. David had numbered all the poles so the framework took no time to assemble. Getting the heavy canvas over the roof was another matter.

The canvas was sodden from all the rain and twice as heavy as usual. It felt like hardboard and was about as flexible. By the time they had got it into position, Ben was cross and wet through. Streams of water from the tent kept slopping down his outstretched arms into his shirt. His shoulders ached and his knuckles were raw in places.

Clipping the tent sides to the frame was easy by comparison. David grinned at him. 'No tourists on this safari,' he laughed. They pushed and pulled the tent into position until it covered the rear of the vehicle. Then David went back on top of the Land-rover and lashed down the tent roof.

'That's to stop leopards getting any ideas,' he told

Ben with a wink. He lit the pressure lamp and pumped it vigorously until the tent was full of warm, friendly light. He put the box of matches back inside a waterproof container and hung the lamp from a hook on the main tent pole.

Ben climbed inside the back of the vehicle and dragged out both camp beds and the wash bowls. Finally, he pulled out the stove.

'You get into some dry clothes,' David suggested. 'I'll put the supper on. How about some of your mother's all-in stew?'

Nothing had ever tasted so good, Ben thought. They wolfed it down and afterwards wiped their plates with hunks of bread. Then they opened a tin of peaches and took it in turns to spear the fruit with their forks.

Ben yawned and closed his eyes. His father was talking and he was trying to concentrate on what he was saying. It was warm and cosy.

The lamp hissed quietly and his father's shadow loomed protectively across the roof of the tent. Whatever might be happening outside, it was safe in here. Ben yawned again. The next thing he knew David was shaking him by the shoulder and grinning.

'Good Morning Campers! Breakfast in five minutes!' He put a mug of tea on the ground beside Ben's camp bed.

'Don't forget to shake your boots out before you put 'em on, in case something nasty's crawled in during the night,' he called.

Ben put both hands round the mug. The air was surprisingly cold. He sipped the hot tea gratefully and listened to the roar of the cooker. It was very soothing. He wanted to slip down under the blanket again and go back to sleep.

But his father's cheerful voice brought him sitting upright instead. 'Did you hear those jackals sniffing around outside an hour ago?'

They ate breakfast quickly and then packed up camp. Ben found it easier than he had expected. Soon they were bumping over grassland towards the swamp. 'Keep your eyes peeled,' David told him. 'Never know what you might see. We'll take it very slowly from now on.'

A few minutes later, David gave a grunt of pleasure. 'Look,' he pointed ahead of them. 'Elephants. Just what we wanted.'

He drove closer approaching them from the side. There was something about the herd that looked familiar. He stared at them intently. Then said, 'I thought as much. They're the ones I saw last week. See the old matriarch. Look at the way her tusks turn in at the ends. Can't mistake her.'

'What are they doing?' Ben asked. 'Why are they all running up and down like that? Have we frightened them?'

'You're right,' David agreed, suddenly concerned and staring hard at the herd. 'Something serious must have happened. Let's go and take a look!'

Seven

They stopped a hundred metres short of the herd and quietly got out. They were on the edge of a steep bank. Five metres below, the ground looked water-logged.

'Must have had a lot of rain yesterday,' David commented. 'Makes the ground round here really dangerous. You get quicksand or bad mud forming.' He broke off and pointed. 'Hey! Look at that elephant!'

Trumpeting loudly, Temba was scrambling down the bank. When she reached the bottom she broke into a shambling run. She began sinking almost at once. After only two strides she was already over her knees in glistening black mud.

'What's she doing?' Ben demanded. 'She's going to get stuck!'

Temba screamed in frustration. The other elephants lining the bank groaned and called to her. David saw fresh mud plastered along their legs and sides.

He pointed at them. 'They've all been down there. What are they trying to do?' he demanded.

Kubwa tossed her head up and down in distress and pounded the ground with her feet.

'Look!' Ben exclaimed. 'That one's still going on.'

Temba forced her way through the mud until it reached the underside of her belly. There she stopped. Physically unable to go any further and shaking with the effort.

She slipped forward and the mud was suddenly up to her chest. She began to flounder.

'Oh my lord!' breathed David Sitole. 'She's not going to get out!'

The rest of the family started to mill around and rush up and down again. There were fresh bellows of panic. With a gigantic effort, Temba began trying to haul herself around.

'If she slips now she's had it,' said David tersely. 'She'll slide straight under.' He stared at her through his binoculars and watched her shoulders hunch.

She groaned with the exertion. There was a loud,

squelching noise as she broke the suction of the mud holding her. Slowly, she pulled a leg free and began to force her way back.

Kubwa came down the bank as fast as she could, screaming for the others to follow. They waded out, seized Temba's trunk and began dragging her to solid ground.

David Sitole had the glasses again. 'I don't believe it!' he gasped. 'There's another one out there. Further out. It's trapped. She was trying to save it! Here! Look!'

Ben's hands shook. All he could see was a mass of churned-up mud. It was hard keeping the binoculars focussed. He thought he could see the outline of an elephant lying on its side and had to look several times to be sure. But by then, the shape of the head and trunk were unmistakeable.

'It's really small!' he shouted. 'It's only a baby!'

An hour ago, as mischievous and reckless as ever, Moto had raced ahead of the family, determined to be the first to get to the new mud wallow the family had found yesterday.

He scrambled and slid down the bank as fast as he could and set off at a run. But the ground under him began to sway and ripple. His feet broke through the crust and he tripped and felt this terrible sucking mud pulling him under.

He lay still now, too terrified to struggle anymore. Every movement he made forced him deeper into the mud. His mouth and trunk were clogged with it. His breathing was laboured. Worst of all, he knew there was nothing he could do to save himself.

He heard Temba's frantic bellow and felt the mud quiver as she tried to reach him. She was fighting with all her strength just as the others had done. But this was her third attempt and Moto could sense the growing despair in her screams.

With an effort, he raised his trunk and called to her. The family watching on the bank heard him and wailed. They stamped their feet in frustration. Moto fell back exhausted and felt the mud creep remorselessly upwards.

'Come on!' David shouted. 'Can't stand here doing nothing. Hop in!'

Ben scraped his shins on the door sill but said nothing.

'This might be a bit scary,' David warned, quickly reversing the vehicle. 'Just sit tight and do exactly what I tell you. OK?' He looked over at Ben and gave him a reassuring grin. Then he gripped the wheel and drove slowly towards the herd.

At first, no one paid them any attention. The elephants were too busy to worry about them. The old matriarch was reaching down to help Temba climb the bank while her two sisters pushed from behind.

The vehicle was only fifty metres away when Kubwa suddenly wheeled round. For a moment she looked blankly at the Land-rover. Then her frustration boiled over. She trumpeted in rage and charged.

Ben shrank back in his seat. He was paralysed with fear. Thirty metres away, the elephant thundered towards them, dust spurting from her feet. Her ears spread wide on either side of her massive head. Her tusks pointed directly at him.

He heard his father shouting and looked at him, uncomprehending. David was pounding his fist on the outside of the door and yelling at the top of his voice. Ben saw that he had jammed a thumb on the horn.

'Noise!' he father was shouting. 'Make all the noise you can!'

Ben opened his mouth but no sound came. His

arms were leaden weights hanging down by his sides. There was nothing he could do.

Helplessly, he watched Kubwa closing in on them. He saw her tusks swing down. Now she was filling the whole windscreen. He could see the deep wrinkles criss-crossing her trunk and a scar on her forehead.

David Sitole's mouth was dry with fear but his brain raced, searching desperately for a way out. This elephant was going to hit them and there was nothing he could do to avoid it. He had been charged before but never with such ferocity.

They jolted over a sudden bump and his hand cracked against the control column. The headlights flashed on and Kubwa threw up her head in sudden fright. She swerved and thundered past less than a metre from Ben's door.

The Land-rover rocked and went up on two wheels. It hung there for an eternity then fell back with a crash that jarred every bone in their bodies.

David recovered first. He spun round in his seat. 'Where is it? Where's it got to?' he shouted, wrenching at the steering wheel. They made a wide turn and saw Kubwa some thirty metres away.

But the old elephant was flagging. The charge

had taken all the energy she had left. She stared at them, her sides heaving and a line of froth showing along her mouth. Her head drooped.

David braked hard and the Land-rover jerked to a halt. 'Sit tight! Don't move!' he ordered. He pushed his door open, stood up on the seat and looked around. There was no sign of the rest of the family.

He breathed a long sigh of relief and got back inside. He felt his body shaking and slumped forward over the wheel. They watched in silence as Kubwa stalked away.

David looked at his son. 'You OK, boy?' he asked quietly.

Ben swallowed and managed a weak smile. He gave a little nod.

'That's what you call a close encounter,' his father exclaimed, taking a very deep breath. He put his arm round Ben's shoulders and held him tight.

'Didn't mean to scare you,' he said.

'It's OK Dad. Honestly,' said Ben, gulping. He looked away and rubbed his nose on his T-shirt. 'Hadn't we better take another look at that little one?'

Eight

They stared down at Moto. 'Why can't we radio for help?' Ben asked. 'They could send a helicopter, couldn't they?'

His father shook his head. 'No point,' he replied. 'He'll be sucked under long before anyone could get here. Besides,' he made a face, 'They wouldn't send a helicopter anyway. Cost too much.'

Ben squatted on his haunches. 'That big elephant, the one we saw,' he said, pointing at the mud. 'She got really close.'

David considered. 'Still a good metre short. There must be a hole out there. The mud starts getting deep all of a sudden.'

'If only we had a ladder or something. Then we could reach him and tie a rope round his legs,'

Ben mused.

David shook his head. 'Ladder's no use. It would sink under me.' He scratched his head. 'We've got to spread the weight out somehow.'

Ben stared at his father. Yes! That was it! Something he had learned in science lessons. Something to do with weight ... And then he had it.

'The tent!' he cried. 'We could use the tent.' David blinked.

'But that's it!' Ben yelled, leaping to his feet. 'Dad! Don't you see? We unclip the sides and spread them out across the mud.'

David stared at him. It wasn't a bad idea ... but ...

'It still wouldn't take my weight.'

'But it would mine!' Ben interrupted. 'Then we can winch him out.'

David Sitole was impressed. The boy might be right. The only trouble was, he could not let him do it. He looked at Ben's shining face.

'I'm sorry Ben. Nice try. But it's way too dangerous. What on earth would your mother say?'

'She'd say, give it a try,' Ben cried. He grabbed David's arm. 'Come on Dad! Let's just see if it works.'

His father hesitated.

'We can't just let the calf die without doing something,' Ben pleaded. 'Just one try. That's all. I promise!'

David stared at his son. He was taken aback by the boy's vehemence. He looked across at Moto and wavered. 'Well . . .' he began. But Ben was already racing round to the back of the Land-rover.

They heaved the tent down and unclipped the sides. 'It'll reach, easy,' exclaimed Ben.

'Let's see if it'll support you first, shall we?' said his father grimly.

'If we roll up the other sides tightly,' said Ben, 'perhaps I can push them in front of me.'

'I must be mad,' David muttered to himself. Then he straightened up and jabbed a finger at Ben's chest. 'We'll try it where the mud's not too deep. If that works . . . then I'll . . . I'll think about it.'

Ben didn't bother to reply. They dropped the rolls of canvas down the bank and followed, sliding on their bottoms.

'Right then,' called David. 'Let's roll it out. You get ready to lie on it.'

Ben edged forwards and felt the canvas sinking beneath him. The sides curled towards him. He crawled on. It got worse. 'It's not going to work!' he shouted. Tears of rage started in his eyes. He wanted to pummel the canvas in frustration.

'Hang on!' David ordered. 'You're doing it all wrong. Pretend you're a frog. Spread your arms and legs right out. Try and touch the corners. That's it!' he called a moment later. 'That's better!'

He waded out alongside Ben. 'Now . . . lift your body. That's it!'

Awkwardly, Ben pushed himself up on to his hands and knees. The canvas wobbled then tilted sharply.

'Spread out!' he heard his father shouting. 'Get all your weight on your hands and feet.'

He did so and some of the shaking stopped.

'Now try moving forward,' David called.

Ben slid a hand a few centimetres forward. He did the same with his foot.

'And again,' his father encouraged. 'Do that again.'

Suddenly, Ben was moving with more confidence.

David watched him in mounting excitement. 'OK! Come back now,' he called. Well, what do you reckon?' he asked as soon as Ben was back on firm ground. 'Think you can you do it?'

Ben thought for a moment and said soberly, 'Yes. Just so long as you've got a safety rope round me, I'll be fine.'

David seized him by the shoulders, wide-eyed with excitement. 'Ben! You're sure? That's wonderful! And remember, the further out you stretch the more support the canvas will give you.'

Ben nodded. 'I know what I've got to do now,' he heard himself say and hoped he sounded more confident than he actually felt.

'We'd better hurry then,' said David. 'Time's running out for that little creature.' He looked up the bank. 'I'll get the ropes and pay out the winch. You stay here.'

It was a stiff climb but David hardly noticed it. The sooner the next half an hour was over, the better. He couldn't believe he was really letting his son do this. He must be mad. Then he looked down at Moto and knew why it had to be done.

He turned the Land-rover round and drove it as near to the edge as he dared. He left it in gear facing out over the mud. He flung two coils of nylon rope down to Ben.

Out of the corner of his eye, he saw Temba move out into the open and guessed she was the calf's mother. She was a hundred metres away. He waved at her. 'We'll do our best!' he shouted and suddenly felt like crying.

Then she was forgotten as he switched on the winch motor. He pulled on a pair of large gloves and seized the tow hook. He took a deep breath and started to drag the heavy wire behind him down the bank.

He spent the next five minutes getting the ropes ready. 'This is the one you'll need to get round its leg,' he explained.

'Get the feel of it,' he ordered. 'Here! Take it. Bend it in your hands. Smell it! We've only got one chance. So let's practise tying the knot. Take it round my waist a couple of times. If the knot slips then that animal is as good as dead.'

When they were both satisfied, David tied the other rope as a life line under Ben's arms. He checked it carefully. 'That won't come off,' he assured the boy.

David put his hands on his son's shoulders and looked at him. 'Just take it steady. Keep your weight spread.' And with his own heart in his mouth, he helped Ben on to the canvas.

'Go get him Tiger,' he whispered.

Halfway across, Ben started to push the next roll

of canvas in front of him. For a dreadful moment, he almost lost his balance and began sliding forwards into the mud.

He didn't hear his father's shouts or feel the increased pressure under his armpits. He was too busy concentrating. He was out on his own now. David was some way behind him. He could feel the mud moving under him. It was not a pleasant sensation.

He tried pushing the roll with his forehead exactly as an elephant would. And to his surprise, it worked. It was slow going but he found it easier to keep his balance. Ben's confidence grew.

He had now got as far as Temba had and the smell of the mud made him gag. There was worse to come. A cloud of small flies found him and settled on his arms and face.

Ben knew he must not on any account let them distract him. They were in his ears and hair and crawling inside his nostrils. The elephant was only a metre away but his arms and shoulders were begining to shake with the strain.

He took a fresh grip on the rope and slid onwards. He kept his eyes firmly on the elephant. Less than a metre to go.

Suddenly, he was full of doubt. Moto's bulk looked huge. Ben realised with a feeling close to panic that he would have to put his face in the mud if he was to get the rope around the elephant's leg.

He fought down the bile that rose in his throat and slid a few centimetres further on.

Nine

Moto knew Ben was there. He had listened to the sound of the boy's breathing getting closer and his eye rolled back in terror. He knew he was drowning. There was nothing he could do about that. But now, Man, the greatest enemy of all, was also trying to kill him.

Moto felt the sudden weight of a human being lying on top of his thigh. New terror gripped him. He struggled to get away with all the strength he had left. His legs stirred feebly then his head flopped back. Liquid ooze slopped into his mouth.

But Moto's terrified struggles had made all the difference. The elephant's back legs moved a couple of centimetres apart. Just enough for what Ben had to do.

The boy closed his eyes and reached down into the mud with both arms. He thought he could feel the end of the rope but it was hard to tell in all the slime. There was nothing for it. He must go deeper.

He moved forward to the very edge of the canvas. He took a deep breath and went face down in the mud, his hands on either side of Moto's leg. Mud like thick soup covered his neck and shoulders. He felt for the rope end again and found it!

He pulled it round under the elephant's leg and brought it to the surface. So far so good! He took another great gulp of air and went back down. He managed to take two more complete turns round the leg and decided that should be enough.

Quite suddenly, he was shaking with fear. He felt totally on his own. He wanted to turn round and look for his father. But he didn't dare. There was a greater terror. And it was out here surrounding him. It was the thought of all that mud closing over his head.

Now he was looping the rope through itself to make the knot. It was almost there. There was a spasm of cramp in his forearm and he had to wait until it had gone.

Now he was pulling the knot tight while the canvas

lurched under him. It slid away and a wave of mud rushed towards him. It covered his shoulders reaching for his mouth. Getting deeper! His frantic hands found Moto's legs and he pushed down hard to keep his head above it.

The rope under his arms tightened and started dragging him steadily back. He slipped and went sprawling while the canvas buckled under him. The mud followed him like a malevolent wave. It had a life of its own.

He had no idea how long it went on for. It seemed to last for ever. Then Ben felt his father's arms around him and he was half-dragged and half-carried to the shore. David was hugging Ben and wiping the mud from his eyes and nostrils.

'Ben . . . I thought we'd lost you!'

But the only thing Ben could think about was the knot. His entire life was bound up in it. Would it hold? It had to! It was the only thing that mattered. He pushed his father's hand away and got unsteadily to his feet.

'Come on Dad!' he cried. 'The elephant! We've got to save the elephant!'

It was just the spur David needed. He looked at Ben and nodded. Without another word, he turned and started climbing the bank. Near the top he slipped and had to grab at a small bush to stop himself falling.

At the top, David received a shock. The same large elephant had moved even closer. She was now barely thirty metres away, silently watching them. She must have seen everything they were doing.

But David had no time to spare wondering. 'Keep clear!' he shouted, waving Ben to stand well away.

The motor hummed and the winch began to turn, quickly taking up the slack. The rope out to the elephant stirred then tightened. It came out of the water like a long black snake.

The noise of the motor grew louder. The rope was taut now like a bow string. Dollops of mud fell from it. There was no sign of movement from Moto. But the knot was holding.

The rope began to arc under the strain. David dug his fingernails into the palm of his hand. The motor whined in protest. 'Please God!' David whispered. 'Oh! Please God!'

There was a loud squelching noise followed by a smothered bellow from Moto. Then another cry from the calf. A panic-stricken scream that went on and on. And for a dreadful moment David thought the rope was tearing off the animal's leg.

There was an even louder sucking slithering sound and then the rope began to move. Jerkily at first. Tugging at the elephant. David's heart was in his mouth, convinced the knot was slipping.

But Ben had done his work well. The knot held and both humans watched incredulously as Moto came out of the mud and began to move steadily in towards the shore. It was a moment of pure joy.

Ben did a dance of triumph while David sang at the top of his voice. He cut the motor and looked up to see that Temba was now even nearer. David didn't wait. He picked up a sharp machete and slid down the bank. Ben followed.

Moto lay on his side, weakly moving his legs and trying to get up. Ben stooped over him using his hands to clear some of the mud away from his mouth. The little elephant's trunk suddenly reached up and touched his arm. Ben stroked his head and felt sudden tears pricking his eyes.

'You're safe now,' he said with an unsteady voice.

'Come on! Hurry!' David called. 'Get that rope off. The mother's up on the bank. The whole herd'll be here in a moment!'

Ben began to cut the rope from Moto's leg using

his penknife right at the end, to avoid injuring the calf.

'He'll be fine now,' David said, as Moto began to lift his head and squeal. 'He needs his mother. Look out! Here she comes!'

By the time they were halfway up the bank, Temba was lifting Moto to his feet and cleaning the mud out of his eyes. The noise she was making was deafening.

By the time they had wound in the winch rope, the rest of the herd were already sliding down the bank towards Moto and his mother.

David looked at his son and shook his head. 'You look a sight!' he said. 'You must be exhausted. I know I am! Let's get clear of the herd, fast.'

They drove towards a clump of thorn trees. 'We need a break,' said David.

Ben leaned against the rear bumper, watching his father brew tea. His legs felt rubbery. It was all he could do to stop his body shaking.

'Here! Try this,' said David handing him a mug. 'There's lots of sugar in it. It'll give you strength.' The tea was scalding hot.

'That was very brave, Ben,' David told him a little later. 'I'm very proud of you. And so will your mother be.'

'Will the calf really be all right?' Ben asked.

David shrugged. 'You can never tell with Nature, but this way – well, at least it's got a chance. Thanks to you! Fancy some biltong to chew?'

He walked round the side of the Land-rover, then stopped. Ben heard him chuckle.

'Come and look at this,' he called. 'Looks like the family's back together again.'

Led by Kubwa, the elephants were walking slowly towards them.

'They'll be wanting the shade,' David said.

'That's the one,' cried Ben. 'See! Hanging on to its mother's tail.'

'Very sensible,' commented David. He picked up his binoculars and studied the family. Then he handed them to Ben and started the engine. 'He should be all right. Now it's time to look after you. We'll spend the night in a village I know, near here. The headman's a good friend.'

As they drove past the elephants, Temba broke away and came towards them. David looked puzzled and slowed the vehicle down to walking pace. 'Just sit quite still,' he cautioned. 'I'm not sure what she wants but she looks quiet enough.'

Temba came very close. She stopped a couple of

metres in front of the Land-rover. Ben looked up into her eyes. They were light brown in colour. They held his. He knew she was looking directly at him. It was an extraordinary sensation.

She came a step closer, towering over them. He heard his father gasp. Her tusks were near enough to touch. Ben kept perfectly still as the tip of Temba's huge trunk reached towards him. It stopped centimetres from the boy's face.

There was wonder in David's voice. 'She's come to say thank you!' He swallowed with emotion. 'She's memorising our scent. Seeing what we look like. She won't forget either of us. You can be sure of that.'

Temba lifted her trunk and trumpeted. Close to, it was a terrifying sound. She trumpeted again and turned away. After a few metres, she broke into a run and David swore he saw her skip to one side in sheer good humour. She rejoined the herd, leaving behind two shaken but delighted humans.

'She likes us! She was saying thanks!' yelled Ben. 'Wasn't she?'

David clutched his head in sheer disbelief. 'Ben! You're one lucky son of a gun! You've seen more in the last twenty-four hours than I have these last ten years!' He seized Ben by the neck and shook him playfully. 'And you know something? You deserve it!'

He put his foot down on the accelerator. 'Let's go! Time to get back to civilisation. I feel a bath coming on!'

Ten

In the middle of nowhere a mobile phone rang. Star put his rifle down and sauntered towards the vehicle. He was in no hurry. He knew who was calling.

His bush jacket lay across the front seat. He picked it up and pulled out a bright yellow satellite phone. It was Star's most prized possession. He smiled at it and rubbed his cheek over its smoothness.

'Yes?' he said.

There was no mistaking Ruhl's voice. 'Did you pick up the stores all right?'

Star nodded. 'Yes.'

'All in working order?'

Star grunted. 'We'll be moving out in three hours' time.'

'No way!' Ruhl rasped. 'I want you off your butts in the next ten minutes.'

Star stiffened. 'So what's happened? What's gone wrong?'

'Someone's talked. That's what,' Ruhl snarled. 'The customs people think we'll be bringing the stuff out in three weeks' time.'

Star cursed. 'None of my boys would say anything. I swear it!'

Ruhl cleared his throat. 'It was the barman. It's been taken care of,' Ruhl said with heavy emphasis. 'He's looking for a new job. One where fingers ain't needed.'

'What about us?' Star demanded.

Ruhl was talking again. 'You've got three days. Get all you can. So go for it! We can make up the rest later.'

'But three days gives me no time ...' Star protested.

Ruhl snorted. 'You've got enough fire power to start a war. Stop complaining. Get on with the shooting!' There was a click as he disconnected.

Star stared at the phone. Then he took several deep breaths to regain his self control. Three days to find a herd of elephants out here in all this emptiness?

They'd probably spend the time digging the vehicle out of loose sand or potholes. He cursed again. There were always problems dealing with Ruhl.

Alvarez came around the side of the vehicle and grinned. He pointed at Star's phone. 'A man could kill for a toy like that.'

Star glared at him and pushed past. The others looked up and saw his expression. Their chatter died away.

'I want us ready to move in twenty minutes!' Star commanded. 'Otherwise none of us is getting paid.'

They stared at him open-mouthed. Briefly, he told them what had happened. Then, 'Make sure you've got a full magazine of thirty rounds on your rifle. And five more in your pouches. Don't leave any mess behind.'

They worked in silence. They knew what to do. Sweat gathered on their faces while they stacked the empty ammunition boxes in the back of the truck. They dowsed the fire with water then flung shovelfuls of earth over it.

Star made a careful search to make sure nothing had been left behind. Twenty-four minutes later, Alvarez drove out. Star and the others sat up on the roof, with bandoliers carrying a hundred extra rounds looped across their chests.

They all knew they were going to need a giant stroke of good fortune. But then, they were the sort of men who made their own luck.

'Yes dear! He's a hero,' David Sitole shouted into the telephone. 'I spoke to Captain Amba at headquarters and he thinks Ben should get a medal!' He laughed and passed the telephone to Ben.

'You'll need to speak up,' he told him. 'It's a bad line.'

For a moment, Ben heard his mother's voice at the other end. Then, it was lost in a burst of interference and the line went dead.

'Never mind,' said his father, replacing the receiver. 'She knows we'll be home tomorrow night. Let's go and thank the headman for looking after us so well.'

The headman was a big jolly man who had insisted they spent the night with his family. Ben had never enjoyed a hot shower so much. The mud had got everywhere. In his hair, in his ears, in between his toes and up his nose.

It had felt wonderful soaping himself all over and

then pulling on clean clothes. The headman had even had the cab and the seats hosed down.

Ben hadn't felt the least bit like a hero yesterday. It had never occurred to him. But when his father's boss had personally congratulated him on the radio for all to hear, the boy had felt an enormous surge of emotion.

Trying to look as nonchalant as possible, Ben shook hands with the headman and the village elders. But all the time, his heart was singing inside him. He had helped save an elephant's life. He was bursting to get back home and tell his mother all about it. His classmates wouldn't believe him of course but, right now, school felt like it belonged to another planet.

Almost all the village had gathered to see them off. Ben waved out of the window until his arm ached. Five minutes later, they were driving along a narrow track filled with deep ruts. Head-high elephant grass grew on either side. It was like being in a long yellow tunnel.

Ben saw a cigarette packet lying at the side of the track. It looked brand new. The bottom half was still covered in cellophane. He was just going to mention it when the Land-rover hit a really deep pothole.

Ben hung on grimly while David fought to stop the vehicle sliding off the track altogether. By the time they had recovered, Ben decided the cigarette packet was not that important.

One of the watchers on top of Star's vehicle gave a sudden cry. He pointed at a tree a hundred metres away then shook Star's arm.

'Go left, Alvarez!' Star shouted and banged his boot on the windscreen. The vehicle turned and began bumping towards the tree.

The man beside Star grinned with delight. Seku had the sharpest eyes of any of them. Soon Star could see for himself. One side of the tree had been stripped of bark. There were deep gouges in the wood that could only have been made by elephant tusks. Small curled up strips of bark lay scattered on the ground underneath.

The man shouted and pointed again. Star nodded. 'Keep going straight,' he told Alvarez. 'And take it easy, Those marks are fresh. There's a herd not far from here. I know it!'

Fifty metres further on they found an uprooted bush and beyond that broken branches. There were droppings everywhere. 'How old?' Star demanded.

Seku squatted down beside one and pushed his finger inside it. He looked up at Star and smiled. 'One hour? Maybe less!'

Star laughed. They had found what they were looking for. It was going to be their lucky day after all.

Star nudged Ron inside and she spun off his finger again. He reached out to grab it but —

'Ow!' Ron muttered.

Star laughed, but Ron stood where they were looking that it was going to be each. But it was difficult —

Eleven

Not long afterwards, it began to rain. Heavy drops the size of grapes fell, kicking up small puffs of dust as they did so. 'Good,' said Star. 'Exactly what we need. They won't hear us coming until it's far too late.'

With the rain came a cool breeze. 'Even better,' Star told his men. 'As long as we stay upwind, they won't even smell us. Time to start walking!'

Alvarez switched off the engine and they got out. 'From now on,' Star told them, 'I want no noise. Not even if you tread on a mamba!'

The men looked at each other and licked their lips. Stepping on a venomous snake was not a pleasant thought and one they needed no reminding of. Star grinned and spread his arms wide.

Obediently, the men took up their positions in an extended line on either side of him. They tried to keep ten metres apart. That way, they could cover the greatest possible distance yet still be under Star's control.

When the last man was in position, Star waved them forward. Like soldiers they cocked their rifles. Now a heavy, steel-tipped bullet was in the breech waiting to be used.

Five hundred metres further on, they halted. Star put his head on one side and listened. And he heard something that made him smile.

Carried on the wind were the unmistakeable sounds of a herd of elephants feeding. His men heard it too. They grinned and silently waved their rifles at each other.

But there was a problem. There was much less cover in front of them than there had been. They would have to use all their bushcraft and experience not to be detected. Star needed to get in as close to the animals as possible.

He had enough firepower to kill the entire herd in one long burst of gunfire. That was the ideal. Then they could pick and choose at leisure which tusks they wanted. Stalking individual elephants took far too long. It could also be extremely dangerous for the hunters.

There was a line of fever trees a little way ahead of them. Star could see their tops and guessed that this was where the elephants were feeding. He stood motionless while the rain streamed down his face, planning the best way to attack.

The men watched him bend double and set out at a run towards a nearby tangle of thorn bushes. Very cautiously, he peered round the side. Although it looked clear, there was always the risk of being spotted by a solitary animal away from the rest of the herd.

Satisfied, he waved the men forward. They came in a short rush and dropped down behind their own selected cover. They knew what to do. They were after all, the best in the business.

Moto would not leave Temba's side. Ever since the incident with the mud, he had clung to her like a leech. Temba had never known him behave like this.

Gone was the mischievous, headstrong calf who was a constant source of worry to her. The Moto who chased wart-hogs or passing wildebeest had disappeared. He was morose and unhappy. Even the other calves had given up trying to get him to play.

Temba saw that he was trembling again. Anxiously, she ran the tip of her trunk over his head to reassure him, then took his little trunk in hers and squeezed it.

She looked round and saw the others were some way ahead of them. Distracted by Moto's listlessness, she had left Kubwa on her own and dropped to the back of the herd.

The rest of the family were also worried about Moto. Temba could hear them talking amongst themselves and making comforting noises to the calf while they browsed. She heard Kubwa calling for her and knew it was time to return to her mother's side.

Moto trotted after her, ignoring the excited squeals of the other calves. They were having a fine old time playing hide and seek in and out of the bushes.

Temba plodded past and saw Kubwa suddenly raise her head and spread her ears wide. Her great tusks glistened in the rain. Temba heard uncertainty in her call. Puzzled, she began to hurry.

None of the others seemed at all concerned. One of Temba's sisters was kneeling down stabbing the ground with her tusks. She sucked up a trunkful of damp earth and blew it high into the air in sheer good humour.

Temba gave her a playful slap as she went past. She would have stopped there longer if Kubwa had not taken an abrupt pace backwards and trumpeted in alarm. The family stopped in its tracks. They lifted their trunks trying to find out what was out there. A flock of parakeets exploded from the middle of a bush and flew screaming into the trees.

Temba was moving quickly. Her concentration centred entirely on her mother. She saw Kubwa stiffen, scream a warning and charge.

Temba pounded after her. Something was terribly wrong. She burst through a clump of bushes and out into the open. And then the day was suddenly full of violence.

There were bright flashes in front of her and the crack of guns. Something red hot ripped through her ear and went howling past. She could smell cordite and the reek of hot oil.

Then she saw Men! Small figures kneeling, crouching and others running towards Kubwa. More flashes now and the ripping sound of automatic rifles.

She heard the thud of bullets hitting bone. Kubwa staggered and nearly fell. Somehow she kept her balance. She was almost on top of the men. She was trumpeting with rage. Then Temba saw blood spouting in a neat line across her forehead. She could smell scorched flesh.

Kubwa was falling. Her head was slipping over to one side. Only her momentum was keeping her upright. Her front legs suddenly gave way and stuck out in front of her like a child's rocking horse. They ploughed great furrows through the soft red earth before she came to a stop.

When she did, she remained upright. Rigid and motionless. Her eyes wide open with shock and the pain. Some part of her brain was still functioning. As the men rushed towards her she tried to push herself back on her feet.

She managed to get one leg under her. One of the men raised his rifle and fired a burst of ten rounds at very short range into her ear.

Kubwa gave a long sad groan and slowly toppled over onto her side. Her legs swung upwards then fell back with a crash. She gave a great shudder and died.

'There's another one!' screamed Star. 'Get it!

Quick!' But Temba was already back in cover and running for her life. Bullets followed her for the next fifty metres, shredding bushes on either side. There was no sign of Moto or the others.

Her lungs felt they were bursting. She ran faster than she had ever run before and all the time two thoughts hammered at her brain. Kubwa her mother was dead. Now it was up to her to protect the family from these terrible men.

'Now that's a pity,' said Star, taking an empty magazine off his rifle. He stuffed it into a pouch on his belt and re-loaded with a new one. He was seething with anger at missing Temba but was doing his best to conceal his feelings.

'We'd have had enough with both of those,' grumbled Alvarez. 'Now we've got to hang around in all this stinking rain.'

'There'll be others,' Star assured him. He stroked one of Kubwa's tusks. 'Nice! Very nice!' he said.

'How heavy do you reckon they are, boss?' Seku asked.

'There's only one way to find out,' Star replied. 'Alvarez! Go get the axes!'

Twelve

The radio crackled. David reached across and turned the volume up. The noise got worse. He shook his head. 'One of these days they'll buy us some new equipment.'

'It worked all right in the village,' Ben reminded him. 'You got through first time.'

'Well it's not working now,' David said crossly. 'The set's old and temperamental.'

'How far are we from headquarters?' asked Ben.

'A long way,' his father told him. 'Four hundred miles. Maybe more.' He jerked his thumb behind him. 'That village back there is the last place on the telephone line. After that, there's nothing. Just a thousand miles of desert.'

They drove in companionable silence for a while,

both preoccupied with their own thoughts.

'What's your favourite animal?' Ben asked suddenly.

His father reflected. 'That's a hard one,' he said after a pause. 'I try and respect all animals.' Then he chuckled. 'But you're right. There are some I prefer.'

'Like elephants?'

David nodded. 'Like elephants. They've got so much dignity and they're really intelligent. They've got feelings just like us.' He looked at Ben. 'Do you know that they mourn their dead?'

Ben's eyes widened.

'It's a fact,' David added. 'I've seen a female elephant broken-hearted when her calf died. She kept touching it and crooning over it for days. Some of the other wardens believe they cry as well.'

Ben thought about this. Then, 'Which animals do you hate?'

David frowned. 'Hate's the wrong word. You shouldn't "hate" any of them. They're all exactly how Nature wanted them to be.'

'Like hyenas?' Ben scoffed. 'How can anyone like hyenas?'

David looked at him and shrugged. 'OK. So

they're scavengers. But that's their job. They also make loving mothers and look after their young really well. That's more than a lot of humans do.'

'They've got strong jaws,' Ben added.

'They have!' David agreed. 'They can crack open elephant bones. And that's something no other animal can do. Not even a lion.'

The sun had reappeared and now the ground steamed in the intense heat. Star squatted down beside Kubwa's head. He ran a hand along her tusk. It was smooth and warm.

'See here, Alvarez,' he called, beckoning the man over. 'There's thirty more centimetres of ivory inside this old cow's skull. And I want it all! So cut it here! And here!'

Alvarez rolled his eyes. He knew exactly what to do. Elephant tusks were like teeth. There was always more of them under the skin. But if Star thought he was some kind of idiot, well, that was fine by him. Perhaps one day Star would seriously underestimate him. And live to regret it.

Alvarez rumaged inside a holdall and selected a heavy knife. For a moment he rested it on Kubwa's wrinkled old hide. It gleamed expectantly. Then using a lot of strength, he made two deep slashes following the bulge of the elephant's tusk. Hot blood splashed over his wrists. He put a hand on Kubwa's cheek to steady himself then started tugging back the skin. Later, he reached for a smaller knife with a serrated edge and began scraping away the flesh until the rest of the tusk showed.

Half an hour went by before he sat back on his haunches, wiped his hands on the back of his trousers and stretched. Then he brushed away the sweat from his eyes with a blood-stained forearm. A cloud of flies buzzed round his head.

Star inspected his work and nodded. 'Be very careful with this next bit,' he cautioned.

Muttering to himself, Alvarez picked up an axe. He ran his thumb over the blade, testing its sharpness. Satisfied, he measured the distance with an expert eye, swung the axe round his head a couple of times and brought it thudding down into the bone. The flies buzzed in protest then greedily settled back.

The rest of the men cheered and shouted encouragement. It took three more swings before they managed to wrench the tusk clear. The others clustered round it, whooping and laughing in delight.

'You beauty!' Star exclaimed, kissing its tip. 'Must weigh thirty kilos easy!'

Seku carried it very carefully in outstreched hands round to the back of the vehicle. He took great care laying it on top of a pile of sacks. Alvarez wrapped a bunch of rags around the tip to protect it still further.

Star looked at his watch and then up at the sky where a pair of vultures was already circling overhead. He kept thinking about the other elephant. The large female that had got away.

How they had missed her he couldn't think. Lack of practice, he supposed. She had good tusks too. Nothing like as spectacular as the old matriarch's but big enough. If they could only bag her as well, Ruhl should be well satisfied.

The more he thought about it the more certain he became. If they hurried now, they should find her. There would be no difficulty following the trail left by the fleeing herd. That would be child's play.

He wanted one more chance to get in close and have a shot at her. This time, they wouldn't miss. He knew it for sure.

There was a shout of laughter from the men. They were lighting cigarettes and boasting how they'd spend their money. Star knew what would come next if he didn't act quickly. Any moment now one of them would produce a rum bottle to celebrate and the rest of the day would be a write-off.

Cursing, he walked back to the dead elephant and shouted for them to join him. Kubwa lay on her side. The hole in her cheek was thick with flies and the smell of blood hung heavily in the air. Her other tusk was partly hidden under the side of her head.

They stood round looking down at her. 'We'll need to get it off,' Star said. He put a hand on Kubwa's trunk. 'As far up as possible. About here!' He indicated.

Alvarez nodded in agreement.

'So what are you waiting for? Television cameras?' Star chided sarcastically.

Alvarez grinned and picked up the axe.

Temba slowed to a walk. A mile further on, she finally stopped beside a huge ant hill. She stood there, flanks heaving, waiting for the pounding of her heart to stop.

Then she put her head on one side and listened. But she could hear nothing sinister. There were no sounds of pursuit. No sudden snap of a twig underfoot nor the rustle of grass in the middle of a still day. Nothing. Just the occasional trill of bird song and the lazy hum of insects.

She raised her trunk and searched the air. A kilometre away, a troop of baboons was squabbling. She could hear the females screaming at each other and the deeper bark of the male leader.

Later still, she heard groaning and muffled bellows. Temba remembered seeing a very old buffalo hiding away in the long grass. It had been dying then. It sounded now as if a lion had found it first.

But there was no sign of the Men. She sighed out loud in relief and for the first time in hours relaxed. She flapped her ears vigorously to cool herself. Her left ear was painful and she remembered the sound the bullets had made and shivered.

They had a power and a malevolence that terrified her. If she closed her eyes, she could hear the terrible howling they made as they went flashing past, and the sickening thud when they hit anything solid.

Temba swallowed. Her mouth was full of dust and she longed for water. It was the hottest time of the day when the humidity was overpowering. Her legs ached and her head began to droop. She was exhausted.

The temptation to close her eyes and sleep was almost irresistible. She knew that no other animal would be moving around at this time of day. And even if they were, none of them could harm her.

No one that was except for Man. Man was unpredictable. And dangerous. Kubwa had always told her that. Now Kubwa had been proved dreadfully right. She had given her life defending her family against him.

Temba heard the scrape of tiny claws on a stone and a faint slithering sound. A mongoose walked in front of her, dragging a freshly killed snake between its front paws. She watched it disappear into a hole in the ant hill. The mongoose did not see the elephant but Temba could smell venom on the snake's lips.

She shook her head and tried to collect her thoughts. She must find Moto, then gather all the family together. There was no time to waste. For all she knew, the calves may have panicked and become separated from the family. To be lost out here was certain death. They would be lucky to survive the night.

Ancient instincts stirred inside her. She was now the leader. It was up to her to bring the family back together again. She was sure the others were still some way ahead of her but not by much. None of them had her stamina or speed.

She knew they would look for the thickest cover they could find and wait there until night came. They would know Kubwa was dead and be uncertain what to do next. They would wait for her to come to them.

Temba yawned. She shook her head at the flies and wearily set off. When the family were all together she would lead them back to that terrible place. They would want that.

As she plodded, she heard the distant sound of a Land-rover. She stopped and followed it with her trunk. She decided it was going away from her and trumpeted after it, in anger.

'Fancy a drive?' David asked.

Ben's eyes gleamed. 'You bet!'

They changed places. Ben sat forward on the seat and gripped the steering wheel tightly.

'Easy does it,' his father encouraged. 'Let the clutch out ... gently!' he broke off and braced himself with a hand against the dashboard.

The Land-rover jerked violently and stalled. 'There's no rush,' David said. 'Take your time.'

With a set face, Ben started the engine again. This time there was much less jerking. He accelerated and changed gear without any trouble.

'Keep it like that,' David called. 'You're doing fine. But watch out for holes.'

They drove slowly for the next hundred metres until David said 'Go a bit faster if you want to. Hey!' he exclaimed a moment later, pointing at the ground in front.

'There's been another vehicle along here. Quite recently. Look how fresh the tracks are.'

'Maybe it's another warden,' suggested Ben who was beginning to relax a little.

David shook his head. 'No one else for miles. Headquarters would have told us.' He rubbed his jaw. 'Oh well. We'll probably meet up with them soon enough.'

They came to a fork in the track.

'Which way?' Ben asked.

David shrugged. 'Might as well follow the man in front.'

Ben swung the wheel and they drove between tall

banks of elephant grass. There was a solitary tree ahead. As they went past, Ben thought he saw a man waiting there. A man with a rifle! He stared at the wing mirror but there was still too much dust to see anything. But there had been someone there. He was sure of it. And with a gun!

His brain whirled. 'Dad!' he yelled and stamped on the accelerator. He heard his father's shout of alarm but by then the wheels had gripped and they went broadside round a bend and jolted out into open ground beyond.

There was another man hiding behind a bush!

For a split second Ben saw him peering at them through the branches. Then he ducked down. But it was long enough! Ben knew that there were others hiding there. He just did. He also knew something was very wrong.

'What are you doing!' David was shouting. 'Stop it! Stop!' He seized the steering wheel and Ben knew he had seen nothing. He tried to scream at his father to look! But nothing happened. No sound came. He was living in a nightmare. For real!

Then the clearing was full of men. Men with guns and coloured handkerchiefs at their throats. One of them lifted a rifle to his shoulder. Ben looked beyond him and saw the great bulk of the elephant lying on the ground.

Then his father's arm grabbed at his shoulder pulling him down. There was a loud bang and the windscreen exploded round their heads. His father was yelling and Ben heard the terror in his voice.

The Land-rover lurched, tipped over to one side and stalled. Ben's door was flung open and a brawny arm reached in and dragged him out.

Thirteen

'Well, well, well!' said Star. 'What have we got here? A big game-warden and a baby game-warden.'

'I'm not a baby,' said Ben and cried out as Seku jabbed him hard in the ribs with the muzzle of his rifle.

'Leave him alone! He's my son,' said David hoarsely. There was blood in his hair and cuts all over his face from the exploding windscreen.

'Let's kill 'em!' snarled Alvarez.

'We will. Quite soon,' Star assured him. He turned to David Sitole and studied him. His own face was expressionless. 'What are you doing here?'

'Taking my son on safari.'

'But why here?' Star questioned. 'Why come to this area in particular?'

'Well . . . the swamp,' David told him. 'It's the best animal place for miles. Everyone knows that.'

Star moved very close to David. There was a knife in his hand and he held the blade against David's neck.

'How long you been following us?'

David swallowed. The pressure of the blade increased. His face began to stream with sweat. 'I swear to you,' he gulped, 'We only saw your tracks ten minutes ago. We just sort of followed them.'

'Plenty enough time to radio your headquarters.' A faint smile crossed Star's face. 'I heard you calling.'

'We're out of range up here,' David said desperately. 'I know that because I tried calling them much earlier. I couldn't get through then. I swear it!' He stared into Star's eyes, pleading silently with the man. 'Oh Lord,' he prayed, 'make him believe me.'

There was no response from Star. His eyes were as cold and merciless as a snake's. There was a long silence before Star nodded to himself as if confirming a fact he already knew.

'Search him!' Star ordered. 'And then tie his hands. The boy as well.'

'They'll only be in the way,' grumbled Alvarez. 'I

say we get rid of them now before they start sending out search parties.'

Star smiled at David. 'My friend here is a man who enjoys his work.'

'You killed that elephant, didn't you!' Ben burst out suddenly. 'You're poachers. And I'm not frightened of you!'

Star stared at him. For a moment he looked taken aback. He walked towards the boy. Ben looked at his father's face and saw he had gone too far.

Star put his hand under Ben's chin, tilting his head up. The boy tried to resist but it was impossible. Star's grip was very strong. He looked down at Ben's upturned face.

'But you should be *very* frightened . . .' was all he said.

He nodded to Seku who seized David by the collar and flung him against the side of the Land-rover. He kicked his legs apart then ran his hands over David's body, deftly removing his wallet and ID card. 'No weapons,' he grunted.

Star nodded. He believed David's story. These people were a nuisance. Nothing worse. 'Tie 'em up!' he ordered. 'Hands in front, so we can see them.'

Ben gasped with pain as the rope bit into his wrists. He jerked his hands away. Then cried out as Alvarez slapped him across the ear.

'Keep still! Or I'll tie your hands so tight your fingers'll burst,' Alvarez grinned.

Star turned away. He walked across the clearing, pulling the yellow phone from his pocket. The number he dialled answered immediately.

'Agreed!' said Ruhl. 'Use them as insurance for the next twenty-four hours. Then get rid of them near the border. Somewhere where they won't be found for a long time.'

Star put the phone back in his pocket. The warden and the boy were now dumped up against the side of the truck. They looked terrified. So they should be. They were of no further interest to him.

He went across to their Land-rover and carefully examined the radio. He checked the frequency and listened carefully. It was working. Wardens were talking but the background static made it impossible to hear what they were saying.

Satisfied, he reached over and ripped out the receiver. He took great delight in throwing it as far as he could into the long grass. Then he walked back towards his own vehicle.

'Time to go!' he called to the men. He bent down towards David. 'I forgot to tell you,' he smiled. 'Any trouble from you and the boy dies first. Understand?'

He straightened up. 'Put them in the back,' he ordered. 'But mind the tusks!'

The truck backfired twice and a cloud of diesel fumes gathered under the tailboard. As soon as it turned out of sight, the vultures began to land.

The elephants returned at midnight. They came silently into the clearing where Kubwa's body lay. They were so quiet that the hyenas heard nothing until Temba came out of the shadows into bright moonlight and walked up to the body.

As the rest of the family followed, the hyenas snarled and slunk away into the tall grass. The family stood round Kubwa in silence. Every line of their bodies showed their distress. Their heads were bowed. Their trunks hung limp. They formed a silent circle around her. The calves felt the tension and stayed close to their mothers, too awed to stray.

Temba caressed the old matriarch's head and face. She ran her trunk over Kubwa's wrinkled skin. She knew every scar and crease in that wise old face. A face that had seen so much of life. The face of a

117

mother, a leader and the best loved friend of them all.

Very slowly, she reached towards the gaping hole in the old elephant's cheek. She knew as they all did why Kubwa had been killed. She shuddered and gave a low, bubbling sigh as her trunk touched the empty socket. The flesh was cold and the blood had dried long ago. The smell of hyena was overpowering.

Temba ran her trunk along Kubwa's lower jaw and over her teeth. She put the tip of her trunk into Kubwa's open mouth in a final act of farewell. The rest of the family groaned and began to move aimlessly about.

Temba turned away. She walked across the clearing and, reaching up, broke off a palm frond. She came back and placed it deliberately across Kubwa's head.

The others followed, some pulling up tussocks of grass or snapping branches. Others kicked at the ground then picked up the earth in their trunks and sprinkled it over the body. They went on doing this until Kubwa's head and trunk were covered.

When they had finished, Temba gave a low call that gathered the family together. She greeted them all in turn. For five minutes, the elephants entwined their trunks, rubbed heads, clicked their tusks together, stamped their feet and ran backwards and forwards, trumpeting.

The family were together again. They had a new leader who would guide them wisely. Satisfied, they followed Temba out of the clearing.

The hyenas watched impatiently from the shadows and bared their teeth. Soon they came stealing back.

But Temba had only gone a short distance when she saw the Land-rover. She stopped in her tracks. Man! Her eyes gleamed with anger. She stamped her foot in warning and the family halted. Her trunk swung towards it.

Carefully, she moved forward and minutely examined the vehicle. She was puzzled. There was something familiar about it. She remembered the two humans she had seen inside.

She stood alongside Ben's door and examined the shattered glass, the bloodstains and the smell. She grew alarmed. These were the humans who had saved Moto. She recognised their scent. But now their blood was spattered everywhere.

There were other scents that made the hairs on her trunk bristle. Dreadful scents of men, different men, mingled with the smell of Kubwa's tusks. And all mixed together so that she knew these were the same men who had butchered her mother.

Temba screamed at the family to remain nearby. She would come back for them. The others moaned in uncertainty and shuffled their feet. They huddled closer and rubbed their heads together for comfort.

Temba began to follow the trail of blood drops. In the moonlight, her trunk left a long wriggling line in the dust as it moved back and forth, following the tyre marks on into the night.

Fourteen

Ben's eyes opened slowly. They were gummy with dust and exhaustion. For a blissful few moments he could not remember where he was. He tried to cling to the dream he had been having. But it began to slip away from him and then reality returned with a rush.

He was very cold. There was a foul taste in his mouth. It was getting light.

Seku and the other man were lying stretched out along the seats. Two empty bottles lay between them on the blood-soaked sacking. The smell of rum, bodies and death made him want to retch.

He turned his head and leant over the tailboard. The pain as the ropes bit into his wrists helped him choke back the nausea. He waited for a while looking glumly at the silent trees, then sank back on to the floor of the truck.

Beside him, David Sitole lay motionless. He was alone with his misery as he took silent stock of the situation. They were prisoners. Captured by ivory poachers. Tied up like chickens on their way to market. And with much the same prospects!

No one knew where they were. No one would wonder what had happened to them for at least another day. By that time the poachers would have disappeared.

The gang had shot another elephant shortly before sunset. It had been a solitary bull with fine tusks. Exactly what the men had been hoping to find. They had cut out the tusks and then celebrated long into the night.

Today, they would be heading back across the border, their mission accomplished. He had gathered that from the men's conversation. All that was left to be decided was what they were going to do with their prisoners.

David had no illusions. He had had all night to think about it. His worry was entirely for his son. Did the boy really understand the danger they were in? Had he any idea of what was going to happen later? Should he tell him? But what would that achieve? Why terrify the boy when there was nothing he could do to save him? He sat up and groaned.

Ben stared at him. He felt totally detached. His mother, his room at home, his friends all seemed from another world. He was looking down now at himself and his father, seeing them both as strangers who had somehow stolen their faces and bodies.

David took his hands and made a brave smile. 'You OK, boy?' They sat together side by side sharing what little warmth they had. The dawn was sombre and the sky grey and heavy.

'Ben! I'm so sorry,' David whispered. 'I've got you into this mess and I can't see any way of getting you out.' He swallowed.

Ben looked at him and saw his father's eyes were full of tears. His own heart filled with misery. He put his head on David's chest and cried. Later, they both felt a little better.

A door in the cab opened and they heard someone rummaging about in front. 'Found them!' they heard Alvarez shout. Soon the smell of cigarette smoke came drifting into the back of the vehicle. Seku gave a loud snore, turned over and went back to sleep again.

'Will they give us any water?' Ben asked. 'My mouth's so dry.'

'I'll ask,' David told him and began shouting.

A couple of minutes later, Alvarez came to see. He scowled up at them. 'Shut up!' he began. Then, 'What you want?'

'Water.'

Alvarez scowled. 'This is not a hotel. You must wait.'

Star appeared. He was wearing his bushjacket against the early morning chill. David appealed to him.

'Please can we have some water? We haven't had any since last night!'

Star shrugged. 'Give them some,' he ordered.

'Can we stretch our legs too, please?' David asked humbly.

Alvarez grumbled and dropped the tailboard with a crash. He made no attempt to help them down. Ben slipped and fell over.

David looked at Star. 'Please untie our hands.' Star ignored him. 'There's nowhere we can run to out here. The ropes are so tight.'

Alvarez returned with a battered looking-saucepan. 'Here's your water,' he told them. 'It's all you're going to get. We're short of it.'

It was the most wonderful drink Ben had ever had. He said so.

Alvarez made a face. 'Don't know why we bother.' He turned to Star. 'It's crazy. There's hardly enough left for us. Why bother with them? They're on their way out.'

David looked from one to the other, understanding exactly what he meant. His blood turned to ice.

Alvarez laughed and took the saucepan from him. He drew a finger across his throat and made a long sucking noise. David's face crumpled. He fell on his knees in the dust. 'Let the boy go,' he begged. 'He can't do you any harm. My son is only twelve. Kill me if you have to. But spare my son!'

'You leave us alone!' Ben suddenly shouted. 'The police will be here any minute. I hope you'll be in prison all your lives.'

Star looked at him and considered. 'A boy with spirit.' He sounded almost pleased. 'I like that in a boy. I like it very much!'

He looked at Alvarez. 'Time to be going. Get them back inside. And wake up those other two animals in there as well.' Alvarez nodded and pulled himself up into the vehicle. He began bellowing.

The truck started and pulled out on to the track with a clash of gears. Choking clouds of dust billowed in over the tailboard. Conversation was almost impossible. Not that David or Ben had much to say to one another.

The nightmare was reaching its dreadful climax. Every mile they drove brought whatever fate Star had choosen for them that much closer.

In the front of the cab, Alvarez was singing. Star sat beside him looking straight ahead. Seku and the other man had gone back to sleep. They had opened a new bottle. It now lay half empty, crammed inside an old army boot.

There was a sudden sharp crack followed by a loud grating noise. Alvarez swore fluently and swung the steering wheel hard over. The sound of grating grew louder. Star was shouting in surprise while the vehicle coasted to a halt. Alvarez pulled at the handbrake and switched the engine off.

He banged his fist on the side of his door. 'Broken half-shaft!' he shouted. 'Broken blasted half-shaft!'

'What's a half-shaft?' Ben asked.

'It's like an axle,' David replied. 'You get them in old vehicles.'

'Everybody out!' Alvarez was yelling.

'You've got a spare, Alvarez?' Star asked.

'Of course! But it's in the back. Under everything else!' the man exclaimed, furiously slamming the door of the cab behind him. He dragged Ben on to the ground. David went sprawling after him. Awkwardly, they got to their feet.

Seku and the other poacher lay dead to the world. Alvarez shook them then raised his fist.

'Stop that you fool!' Star cried. 'Leave them! They're no use. Here! I'll help you unload.'

Alvarez tripped on the sacking and went sprawling. 'Mind the tusks!' Star screamed.

Ben and David watched as they carefully unloaded the four huge tusks. They laid them on the ground and threw the pile of sacks after them. Then they stood looking at the back of the truck.

Alvarez had stowed the jack under a rear seat. It didn't take long to pull it out and manhandle it round to the damaged front axle.

But getting at the replacement half-shaft was a different matter. The new axle was under a pile of stores. It had been the first thing Alvarez had packed.

Star took off his jacket and laid it on one of the

seats. He looked out and saw David watching him. Some of his composure had left him.

'Don't even think of running away,' he snarled. 'Because if you do, we'll come after you. Alvarez is an expert tracker. He'll find you and when he does, you won't be running anywhere, ever. Understand?'

Ben watched Alvarez and Star begin the long job of replacing the shattered axle. When they had pushed the jack in place, they took it in turns to loosen off the wheel nuts. The nuts were old and had been there for a long time. They were not going to come off easily. The two men were soon absorbed in what they were doing.

Ben looked at the other poachers. All he could see was their feet. They were both dead to the world. And it was only then that he remembered. The thought of it made him giddy. He caught his breath. For a moment, everything in front of him seemed to flicker. He leant against the side of the truck feeling sick with excitement and with fear.

But it was a chance! Their only chance. He was under no illusion now. His father would know what to do. Deliberately he turned his back on Star. This must not be overheard. 'Dad!' He had to speak quietly. 'Dad!' his voice trembled. 'Listen. It's important!'

And now a surge of hope was swelling inside him. Ben's eyes gleamed. His voice shook. David was looking at him, puzzled.

'Dad,' he said again. 'The penknife. The one Mum gave me. I've got it! I've still got it on me!'

Fifteen

David stared at him blankly.

'The knife Dad. The knife! It's in my back pocket!'

David blinked. Of course. The penknife. He remembered. His mouth opened in shock. He tried to speak. He looked past Ben to where Alvarez was jacking up the front of the vehicle. Star squatted beside him.

He licked his lips. Ben saw his shoulders straighten and the expression on his face change.

'Get out of sight!' David hissed. 'Walk behind the truck. Slowly!' The world held its breath. But no one called after them. David fumbled for the knife and almost dropped it in excitement. Then it was lying in the palm of his hand, shiny and new and innocuous.

But when he tried to prise open the main blade his fingers were too swollen. He tried three more times. 'I can't do it,' he muttered.

'Let me try. Hold it tight!' Ben ordered. The boy slid a finger nail into the groove at the back of the blade and pulled. The pain made him wince and he stifled a cry. For a moment he thought the whole nail was being torn out.

'It's the rope. It's stopped your blood circulating,' said David.

Ben gritted his teeth. He had to try again. He couldn't give up now. It took him two more attempts before the blade moved.

'It's coming! Go on Ben!' David gasped.

Ben kept pulling. Slowly the blade opened a little further, then stopped. More nail tearing pressure and it swung out half way. David gently took it from him and pulled it right out. It looked ridiculously small.

'You first, Dad!' said Ben, taking the knife back. The rope was new and very hard. Ben's hand was shaking and the blade kept slipping. It took an eternity to make any impression.

Then they heard Alvarez calling. And froze. Unable to think what to do. Seconds passed. They waited for the rush of feet. For Star's voice and the feel of his knife at their throat. Alvarez began swearing and they realised he was only cursing the vehicle.

Slowly, the blade began to bite. It cut through the first strand of rope. They could hear Star talking to Alvarez. It was all so unreal. It sounded as if the poachers were in the next door room. A room with the door wide open. A door which either of them could step through at any moment to see what Ben and his father were doing. Beads of sweat stood out on David's brow.

They heard a cab door slam, then silence. Ben closed his eyes. His life might be over in a matter of seconds. Silently, he began counting. 'Ten . . . nine . . . eight . . .' No one came.

And then the knife was through and Ben dropped it, his fingers rigid with cramp. David did not wait. Pressing down with all the force he could exert, he sawed through the ropes holding Ben's hands. It did not take long. The rope was thinner and worn in places.

David flung out his arms and gave Ben a quick, fierce hug. 'Come on!' he whispered. 'Stick right behind me.' And he was off, bending low and running. A bird screeched a warning and flew out of a bush in a whirl of colour.

Ben turned to follow. As he did so, he looked up at the truck and saw Star's jacket neatly folded on a seat. Without quite knowing why, he reached up and pulled it down.

It was still warm from the man's body and just touching it made him feel even more terrified. But unknown forces urged him on. His fingers closed round the mobile phone. It fitted so snugly into his hand. Then he was running for dear life into the undergrowth.

They stopped for breath, hanging on to trees for support while the blood pounded in their temples. They listened for sounds of pursuit but heard nothing. The forest was very quiet. Ben saw a monkey staring down at him and guessed they were being watched by a hundred other eyes.

David put his hands on Ben's shoulders. 'I want to stay close to the track,' he told him. 'In cover, like this. If we get split up you just keep following it back to the village. And get help. Understand?'

For the next kilometre the going was easy. They ran at a steady jog between clumps of trees and patches of low grass. But all too soon they came to the edge of the forest. Ahead of them was open ground dotted with small scrubby thorn bushes.

They ran on for another ten minutes then paused for breath. David looked back and his heart sank. He could see their tracks quite clearly. There were large patches of sand everywhere. Soft sand which they couldn't help sinking into up to their ankles.

But what was he to do? If he and Ben tried to zigzag round the sand, that would use up precious time and increase the risk of being spotted. If they went straight across it, however, it would not be too long before Alvarez found their tracks.

At any moment the hunt would begin. Perhaps even now, the men were after them, already running through the trees with murder in their hearts. David knew Star would come looking for them. He had not the slightest doubt. And when he found them he would kill them. It was as simple as that. So what was he to do?

About a kilometre in front of them, there was a ridge. David studied it. It was covered with bushes and the occasional outcrop of rock. It was the best cover for miles and with a bit of luck, the country beyond might be equally as good. The only problem was that there were not many places to hide before then.

David took a deep breath. He had decided. To stay out here meant certain discovery. This other way, at least gave them a fighting chance.

'Head for the ridge,' he panted and they started off again. The elation David had felt earlier was rapidly draining away. As he ran, he wondered if all they had really done was to bring forward the inevitable.

He had no idea how time was passing. The poachers had stolen his watch the day before. He looked back again and saw the scuff marks their shoes were making in the sand.

He tried to thrust these thoughts far away from him. All his concentration must be focussed on getting to the ridge without being seen. He owed it to Ben for heaven's sake!

Ben was running alongside him, tugging at his arm. He was holding Star's mobile phone and gesticulating with it. 'Not now. Later,' David gasped pushing away the boy's hand.

Now the ridge was high above them, the trees along its top a dark line against the clouds. They were plunging into dense cover, shouldering their way through bushes and young trees. They had made it! And no one had seen them!

David came to a halt and began sucking in great gulps of air. Slowly he recovered and grinned at Ben.

'Dad!' Ben pleaded. 'What about the phone? You can call headquarters and tell 'em what's happening!'

David's chest heaved. He looked at Ben then back at the mobile. At last he understood. He closed his eyes and grinned. 'Fantastic,' was all he could say.

'Come on then! It's easy.'

'You do it,' David shook his head. 'I'm no good with those things.'

'They're all the same,' Ben was explaining. 'Look! This is how you switch it on . . .' And then they heard voices. Angry voices. Men calling to one another. Poachers, looking for vengeance, casting round, searching for their tracks. And only about a kilometre away, David thought, his heart thumping madly.

Ben stared at him in horror. His face crumpling as understanding dawned on him. 'Quick! What's the number?' he gasped.

David Sitole put a hand to his head. His brain reeled. He couldn't think any more.

'Dad! The number?'

'I can't . . . I can't remember!' he whispered. He shook his head in despair and let his hands fall to his sides.

They heard Star's voice! Calling, from not very far away. There was no mistaking it. 'Where are you little boy? Where are you? We're coming for you . . .'

Oh my God, thought David. Then, out loud. 'Come on Ben. There're rocks and trees up there. They'll never find us!'

They scrambled up the ridge. It was much steeper than it looked. Soon they were both out of breath. They crouched down behind a bush.

A sudden movement caught Ben's attention. A branch swayed. And Alvarez stepped out into the open a hundred metres away.

David's hand gripped Ben's shoulder. 'Keep absolutely still,' he breathed.

Alvarez looked carefully around him then squatted down and examined the ground. He picked up a handful of sand and let it sift through his fingers. He looked up at the ridge and seemed to stare directly at them. David felt the hair on the back of his neck standing up. One movement from either of them and Alvarez would see and know.

There was a very long pause while Alvarez scanned the ridge. They heard him clear his throat and saw him spit. Still they remained motionless. He got to his feet and began walking slowly away. Ben hardly dared breathe. Beside him, he could feel his father's whole body beginning to shake.

Alvarez had his head down looking at the ground, searching for clues as to where they might be. Ben and his father were being hunted like animals.

Alvarez was moving to his right now and away from where they had climbed the ridge. Every step he took lessened the risk of his finding them.

And then the telephone rang!

Sixteen

The phone rang again and went on ringing. Ben jerked it out of his pocket. It fell at his feet and he leapt back in horror. Alvarez spun round with a yell of surprise.

Still it rang. It was the cruellest blow fate could deal them. They had been so close to escaping. And now this. This shrill betrayal. This death knell.

Already, Alvarez had pinpointed its source. He saw the bushes shake as David and Ben began to scramble up the side of the ridge. He gauged the steepness of the slope. They would never make it to the top before he caught up with them. He patted the knife at his belt and began to run.

David looked up and knew this was the end. There was nowhere to go. Only into the trees on the skyline. He looked down past Ben. Alvarez was less than fifty metres away.

David struggled on, his outstretched hand pulling Ben up with him. His foot slipped on a scree of loose stones and for a moment he lost his balance. He fell two metres before Ben helped break the fall. By that time, Alvarez had narrowed the gap by another five metres.

And then Alvarez gave a shout of pain. He stopped and began waving his arms round his face and head. He blundered off to one side trying to get clear of the wasps' nest David had disturbed minutes earlier.

David felt a surge of hope. He was suddenly full of energy. He tugged at Ben's hand, desperately trying to encourage the boy. He was too breathless to call out loud. Above his head, the trees were dark and inviting. Could they still find somewhere to hide? Was there really time?

But at that moment, he saw something move up there. Something just inside the line of trees, watching and waiting for them. He stared at the shadows in horror while his legs became leaden and his strength deserted him.

He stared again and moaned in disbelief. He went

down on one knee. He was beaten. It was too cruel. Star must have got there first. But how could he? How? And did it really matter?

Close behind, Alvarez gave a shout of triumph. He pulled the knife out of its sheath, put back his head and laughed. 'The boy first!' he shouted. 'That's what we promised.'

Ben wanted to run. In his imagination he was already miles away, leaping and jumping over obstacles, never tiring. Running into his mother's house, safely into her arms.

Only he wasn't. He was standing on this hillside instead, his feet rooted to the spot, twenty metres from the man who was going to cut his throat. And there was nothing he or his father could do about it.

Alvarez stopped and looked at them. He wanted to savour the next few minutes. There was no opposition. No one to stop him doing what he enjoyed doing best. He didn't mind very much whether it was an elephant or a man. He licked his lips, looked up and the smile on his face slowly faded.

Temba had come silently out of the trees. She was looking down at them. She had watched the humans climbing towards her and had recognised their scent. She could also sense their fear. They were afraid of the other human following them. They were in danger from this man.

She raised her trunk towards Alvarez. He smelt of blood. Old blood. But elephant blood nonetheless. There was no mistaking it. She caught the smell of oil and exhaust fumes and her anger grew.

She kicked at the ground and spread her ears wide. She lifted her trunk high over her head and screamed. It was an ugly frightening sound. It was a cry that could only have one possible meaning.

She came forward down the slope, rumbling with menace. Ben felt the ground shake as she went past. He felt his father's arms around him but could not take his eyes off the elephant.

Alvarez stood his ground at first. He waved his arms over his head, shouting at the animal, hoping to frighten it. Then his nerve broke and he turned and ran. Temba did not slacken her pace. She came on at a steady walk.

Alvarez raced down the hillside and out through the bushes on to the plain. They could hear him shouting snatches of long forgotten prayers jumbled up with curses and screams for help.

Alvarez was running for his life. Temba followed, keeping a couple of metres behind him. Alvarez kept staring over his shoulder, looking up at his particular destiny. Temba was pushing him to the limits of his endurance.

He began to flag. They saw him stumble but recover in time to avoid Temba's approaching feet. She moved closer, towering over him.

They saw her trunk curl upwards then come swinging down like some gigantic bat. They heard the crack quite clearly and watched Alvarez's lifeless body hit the ground like a rag doll many metres beyond.

Temba turned and ran towards the ridge screaming in delight. She stopped and lifted her trunk at them and trumpeted again. Then she stalked majestically towards the bushes and began to browse.

There was a very long silence. At the end of it, Ben and David hugged each other. Then, exhausted, David sat down and closed his eyes. Ben looked at him and quietly backed away. He had just had a brilliant idea.

He retraced his footsteps down the slope. The wasps were still flying around and he took great care to avoid them. He found the mobile phone without too much trouble. 'Dad,' he shouted. 'Come on down. There's something we must do, right now.'

He waited until David had joined him then tapped in a number. They waited. At the other end a phone rang five . . . six . . . seven times. At last, someone picked up the receiver and said, 'Hello?'

'Hannah! It's Ben!'

There was a silence.

'Hannah! Get Mum quick!'

'Why are you shouting so loud?' Hannah asked.

'I must talk to Mum. It's urgent!'

'I took all your coloured pens yesterday . . .' Hannah began.

David grabbed the phone from him. 'Hannah! It's your Dad. Hello baby! Please ask Mummy to come and talk to me right now! It's very very important.'

'I'm wearing a new dress. Mummy made it for me . . .'

Then came a fresh voice. 'Mrs Sitole speaking.'

'Gloria!' said David his voice shaking with emotion. 'Listen very closely. We've been in big trouble. We're OK now. But you've got to help us!'

Mrs Sitole gave a little scream. 'Is Ben all right?'

'He's fine,' said David looking at his son. 'But there may be poachers still around. So listen hard.'

She did. She listened in silence as David gave her all the vital information he could think of. 'Tell them the men are armed and very dangerous.'

'But what about you?' she demanded, trying desperately to keep the panic out of her voice.

'We'll be OK,' he assured her. 'We're going back to the village. It's only about ten miles south of here. But Gloria! Hurry dear. Please hurry!'

Ben switched off the mobile. 'Great safari, Dad,' he said trying to sound casual.

'And it's not over yet,' David said soberly. 'We're still in big danger. Where's Star got to? He'll kill us if he finds us. You just keep your eyes and ears skinned.' Father and son looked at each other and nodded.

David looked at his watch. 'Let's get started. It's going to be a long hot walk back to the village.'

They scrambled down the slope. 'Stay close,' warned David.

'What about Alvarez?' Ben asked. 'Shouldn't we go and find him?'

His father made a face. 'What for?' he said simply.

Temba watched them leave and decided to follow them. The scrub was high and she moved silently.

The humans had no idea she was so close.

She saw them plod through a patch of deep sand. The man put out his hand and pulled the boy along. Temba wondered why they made no effort to avoid it. She could see an easy way round.

They were a mile from the ridge when Temba realised they were no longer on their own. They were being followed. Somewhere close, there was a lion tracking them.

She stopped and looked up. And saw the vultures circling overhead. They had spotted Alvarez's body. Temba knew that lions also watched the vultures. They would know by now that the scavengers had found a kill. This lion could be on its own or a scout for a large pride. Either way, the humans were in great danger. She broke into a trot.

Some sixth sense alerted Ben. He spun round, cried out in shock and stumbled. He felt David's arm across his body, pulling him close. David was shaking. Sweat pouring down his face.

The elephant was ten metres away. Her huge bulk dwarfed them. It grew bigger and blacker against the sky. It filled their world. They stared at it rigid with fear.

There was no hiding place. Nowhere to run to. It

was too late now for anything. They were at the mercy of a wild animal . . .

Seventeen

The seconds passed. Ten . . . twenty . . . a minute.
Elephant and humans stared at one another. They
could see the flies clustering greedily at the corners
of her eyes. Temba flapped her ears. It was
deafening. Like the crack of a rifle. Or the end of
the world.

Temba was puzzled. She saw panic in their faces.
And smelt it on their skin. The humans were
terrified of her. But she couldn't understand why.

She found a small pebble. She turned it over a
couple of times then flipped it towards them. It
landed just in front of Ben. He did not move.

She found another stone. This time it hit David
on the back of the hand. It lay gleaming in the sun.

As if in a dream, Ben stretched out his hand.

Slowly, daringly, his fingers closed over it. Far away, he could hear David's voice. It was very loud but the words were gabbled and he couldn't understand them. All his concentration was centred on that pebble.

He looked up at the elephant. And the instant he threw it back, he recognised her. Temba's trunk curled and caught the stone before it hit the ground.

He felt his father's arms go limp and heard his incredulous laughter. He realised then that David had been praying for them at the top of his voice.

A little later, they set out again. Temba walking beside them. With each pace their confidence grew. It seemed a miracle. David could only shake his head and marvel.

This huge elephant could kill them both with a casual flick of her trunk. She had killed Alvarez as easily as people swat flies. She could spear them with her tusks or crush them into the ground with one massive foot. And yet, instead, here she was shepherding them back to their own species, in perfect safety.

Only a cowardly shot from a high-powered rifle could kill her. David remembered Star and shivered. He began looking for possible places where the man might still be waiting. But as the miles slowly passed he saw nothing.

They plodded on under the immensity of the African sky. Two small insignificant dots of humanity and an elephant. The only sound was their laboured breathing and the occasional rumble from Temba.

At last, in mid-afternoon, they came to a track. There were tyre marks and in the ditch an empty beer can. They followed it for another half an hour. Then Temba stopped. She could smell dogs and hear them barking. They were animals she disliked intensely.

'We must be getting near the village,' David guessed. 'She doesn't want to go any closer.'

Temba stood uneasily, shifting her weight from one foot to the other. She shook her head. Her meaning was clear. She began to turn.

'She's going!' Ben cried. 'She mustn't. She saved our lives! How can we thank her?'

Temba sucked up a trunkful of dust. She blew it high into the air and sighed.

Ben took a step towards her. Then another. Temba's head swung down and bent towards him. Once again, he looked into her friendly brown eyes.

He gulped as his own eyes prickled, then flooded with tears. They trickled scorching hot down his cheeks. He put out his hand. It was shaking uncontrollably. He tried to speak but his voice choked. His mouth was suddenly full of salt.

Temba reached down and touched his fingers. The tip of her trunk was cool and smooth. He felt it brush his chest. Her breath was on his face. Like a butterfly kiss. It was so tender.

He stood with his head bent, crying as he had never done before. His heart breaking, knowing he would never see this wonderful giant again.

He reached up and gently took her trunk in both hands. He pulled it towards him. It was warm and rough and he thought it was trembling a little.

'Thank you . . . We love you!' was all he could say.

And then she was moving down the track and away from them. Forever. They watched her through their tears until she was out of sight. But she never looked back.

'She's gone to find her family and lead them,' David muttered. 'They'll be needing her very badly. It's the right thing.'

'But what about Star and those men? And all the other poachers!' Ben burst out. 'What about that?'

David did not reply. Instead, he put his arm round the boy's shoulders. There was nothing he could say.

As they approached the village they dried their eyes. Not long after they got there, the helicopters came swooping in. There were two of them.

The police had found and arrested the two drunken poachers without any difficulty.

But of Star, there was no trace.

Later, as the sun began to slide down the sky, the helicopter taking them home lifted off in a storm of dust. It climbed above the village, leaving behind cheering children and a pack of demented dogs.

Ben pressed his face to the perspex window and stared down. The pilot circled round until they found the path Temba had made through the tall grass.

The helicopter climbed still higher. The trail led to a jumble of boulders half covered with trees.

'Please circle once more,' Ben begged. 'I think I can see her!'

The pilot did so. But the light was fading. Was that Temba standing there motionless? Waiting for this noisy machine to go and leave her alone? Or was it just a pile of darker coloured rocks?

'Got to go now,' the pilot's voice broke in cheerfully over the headphones. 'Suppertime soon!'

The roar of the engine grew louder. The helicopter's nose dipped and their shadow began racing away in front of them across the scorched earth.

Ben gripped his father's hand. 'We'll never see her again. Will we?'

David swallowed and bit his lip, hard. He looked at Ben and shook his head. 'No, son,' he said. 'Life never quite works out the way you'd like it to.'

Also by Geoffrey Malone, from Hodder Children's Books

WOLF!

Marak is the leader of a pack of timber wolves, fighting for survival in the worst winter in memory, moving south in desperate search of food.

Ed and Jessica Viccary are newly-arrived in Elliot Lake, Wyoming. Their parents are vets serving the local ranchers.

But when the wolves and the ranchers collide, bloodshed is inevitable.

The Viccarys' love of wildlife draws them into this ferocious struggle with devastating results . . .